"I've listened to your arguments, Brink, but you haven't heard all of mine," Hilary said.

"Go ahead then, I'll listen," he promised.

Hilary opened her mouth to speak, then closed it. Fighting Brink Claiborn was more than difficult, it was next to impossible. She knew she should stick to business, but whenever she came close to him something strange happened. It was like stepping into a magnetic field: the attraction was impossible to see, yet the force of it was overwhelming.

Brink drew a sharp breath and his eyes narrowed as he gazed at her lips. "Want to kiss or talk?"

Startled, Hilary took a step back while her face flushed with embarrassment.

He watched her closely. "You want to kiss," he said softly. "I can see it in your eyes . . . read it on your lips."

"But we don't agree on anything," she protested.

"We agree on this completely," he said, leaning closer. His lips touched hers and magic exploded in a tempestuous flame that scorched like a desert sun. . . .

WHAT ARE *LOVESWEPT* ROMANCES?

They are stories of true romance and touching emotion. We believe those two very important ingredients are constants in our highly sensual and very believable stories in the *LOVESWEPT* line. Our goal is to give you, the reader, stories of consistently high quality that may sometimes make you laugh, sometimes make you cry, but are always fresh and creative and contain many delightful surprises within their pages.

Most romance fans read an enormous number of books. Those they truly love, they keep. Others may be traded with friends and soon forgotten. We hope that each *LOVESWEPT* romance will be a treasure—a "keeper." We will always try to publish

*LOVE STORIES YOU'LL NEVER FORGET
BY AUTHORS YOU'LL ALWAYS REMEMBER*

The Editors

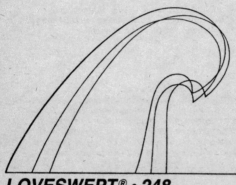

LOVESWEPT® • 248

Sara Orwig
The Object of his Affection

BANTAM BOOKS
TORONTO • NEW YORK • LONDON • SYDNEY • AUCKLAND

THE OBJECT OF HIS AFFECTION
A Bantam Book / April 1988

LOVESWEPT® and the wave device are registered
trademarks of Bantam Books, Inc. Registered in U.S. Patent
and Trademark Office and elsewhere.

If you would be interested in receiving protective vinyl
covers for your Loveswept books, please write to this address
for information:

Loveswept
Bantam Books
P.O. Box 985
Hicksville, NY 11802

ISBN 0-553-21888-3

Published simultaneously in the United States and Canada

Bantam Books are published by Bantam Books, Inc. Its trademark, consisting of the words "Bantam Books" and the por-
trayal of a rooster, is Registered in U.S. Patent and Trademark
Office and in other countries. Marca Registrada. Bantam
Books, Inc., 666 Fifth Avenue, New York, New York 10103.

One

The day should have been wonderful, since there was bright sunshine in the blue sky over Los Angeles. A brisk breeze rolled in from the Pacific during the early March morning. It was weather to make people take note, to make weathermen smile, to make spirits rise. But the beauty of it was lost to Hilary Wakefield because her frustration and anger were causing her temperature to soar several degrees higher than the air around her.

She was parked near a sprawling, redbrick building with a modest sign reading, Delmar Brick Company. The building was new and had a well-tended lawn with sprinklers going, but beside it to the east she found what she was seeking—men and machinery at work.

Bulldozers were parked on brown earth that was covered with bits of rock and debris. In the center of the lot stood a two-story redbrick building, an empty shell with windows and doors gone. Surrounding the east and the south sides of the lot were brick walls, the street bordered the north, and an improvised dirt parking lot filled with workers' cars bounded on the west side. Hilary stepped out of the car, halting when she reached a wire barrier that read, CAUTION! NO TRESPASSING! HARD-HAT AREA.

Her gaze swept the landscape, the big yellow bulldozers, the men in soiled jeans and hard hats. Then she stared at their boss, the only man dressed in a suit. Frustration built up inside her like steam in a boiler when she thought of his hostile receptionist, the unanswered messages, his stubborn refusal to have one more word with her or her family!

He was obviously in charge. Dressed in a navy suit, he waved his hand as if giving directions to two men dressed in jeans who stood with him next to a pile of bricks. His profile was to her, his skin pasty white compared to the men he was with. No wonder he was pale, she thought contemptuously; it came from sitting in his office giving orders and arrogantly refusing to discuss a problem with two little ladies from Mississippi. Brink Claiborn, owner and president of Claiborn Industries, Incorporated, Landfill and Compaction, was so preoccupied with business, he'd tuned out the rest of the world.

Determined to have a word with Mr. Claiborn before she had to return to Mississippi, Hilary stepped over the wire and proceeded carefully across the broad lot that was strewn with bits of wire and broken pieces of glass. She assumed the planners intended to level this lot to use it for parking.

"Hey! Lady, you can't come in here!"

With her green-eyed gaze fastened on her objective, she ignored the shouted warning and kept walking, speeding up her step, thinking Brink Claiborn must be as difficult to reach without invitation as the president of the United States.

Standing in the warm sunshine, the man who had yelled watched her tilt her chin slightly higher and keep walking. When she ignored his call, his first jolt of surprise changed to annoyance, combined with healthy male appreciation. Her legs were long and shapely, her golden hair swung saucily with each step, the narrow skirt of her red dress switched across an enticing derriere that made him momentarily forget she was trespassing. Whatever she wanted, she seemed mighty determined to get it, he thought with reluctant admiration. But he had to stop her before she got herself into a bushel of trouble. He hurried after her, trying to recall the last time he had yelled at a woman . . . and the last time he had been ignored by one. "Hey!" he shouted.

Hilary quickened her pace. In seconds she heard the crunch of footsteps behind her, and then a man spun her around. She faced blazing blue eyes—eyes as blue as the spring sky above—a dirt-smudged face that needed a shave; broad shoulders; bulging muscles beneath a tattered, dusty T-shirt; and a stubborn jaw.

"I intend to have a word with your boss, so save your breath," she said quickly. "He's put me and my family off, time and time again!" she said, her frustration slipping into open fury.

"This is a dangerous area, and you don't belong inside the barricade. Didn't you see the sign?"

"Yes, I did, but I'm going to talk to your boss if it's the last thing I do."

"And it just may be if you don't watch yourself.

Okay, talk," he snapped, frowning. "I'm the boss. Tell me what the problem is."

Hilary had been forestalled by Brink Claiborn's receptionist, intercepted by his secretary, rudely cut off the phone by his housekeeper, and now probably was going to have to tangle verbally with a rough foreman of Claiborn's work crew who intended to run interference for him. She was dangerously close to losing her control. Both aunts had fussed and told her not to do anything impulsive when they had kissed her good-bye in Mississippi, but she was going to lose her cool if she wasn't granted an audience with Mr. B. Inaccessible Claiborn immediately!

"I didn't come all this way to talk to you. Thank you, anyway," she said as witheringly as possible. "I want to talk to Brink Claiborn, that man over there." She pointed to the man in the navy suit. And, mister, no one's going to stop me!"

"Is that so?" The worker's voice no longer resonated with annoyance but with amusement.

"That's right. That man has avoided me long enough."

A lopsided grin tugged at the corner of his mouth, revealing white, even teeth. "Don't you think it would be wiser to call for an appointment and see Claiborn at his office?" His gaze drifted slowly down over her tailored cotton dress.

His scrutiny made Hilary tingle all over. As his smoldering blue eyes lifted to meet hers, she felt an impact to her midsection that was doubly amazing. Aggravation over his boldness and her reaction to him merely compounded her fury.

"An appointment?" she scoffed. "With an arrogant, stubborn man who won't take a call from someone he doesn't care to see? Fat chance. He won't even answer my letters. So what would you do if you needed to talk to him?"

He pursed his lips, and his eyes developed a twinkle that intensified her anger. "I don't think he's more than your average garden-variety stubborn. And if he knew *you* were trying to reach him, I'm sure he would take the call in a flash." His voice suddenly developed a friendly note. "Look, I'm the boss. I'm the man you want to see."

"That won't work!" she said with more curtness than before. She realized she faced another employee who would block unwanted people from seeing the Big Man! "His receptionist has put me off, his secretary has all but told me to get lost, his housekeeper said he refuses to see or talk to me at all. But I have something important to discuss with him. They didn't stop me—and neither will you!"

With a glance at the man in the suit and then back to her, the worker tilted his head. "I'm Brink Claiborn, and you're . . . ?"

"Nice try, but it won't work. I've heard everything. His secretary even told me that Claiborn was out of town, in Europe for the next six weeks—"

"Cindy said that to you?"

"Yes. Europe! And he's right here, fifty yards away. Now get out of my way."

He grinned at her, but he didn't budge an inch, and her temper rose a notch higher. Her voice became quieter, a storm warning her family would have recognized. "You can flex your muscles and throw me out of here, but I'll come right back like a boomerang."

"He can have you arrested for trespassing."

"Wouldn't that make great public relations for his company? I'd welcome the chance to lambast him to the world for his actions—and not just for refusing to see me! I don't think he would want what I have to say to him made public. It would reveal his hard-heartedness!" She fumbled in her purse and pulled out some bills, rolling them in her hand swiftly. "Here, buy yourself a few beers after work and turn your back. He'll never know you talked to me because he's too obtuse to notice anything going on around him!"

"Whoo!" He folded his arms across his chest, making her momentarily aware of the bulge of hard muscles. "You really have it in for the man. Sure you haven't met him before?"

"No, I haven't, but I'm going to meet him this morning." She held out her hand with the corners of the bills poking out from her doubled fist.

He made no move to take them but continued to grin at her. "How can you be so fired up if you don't know him?"

"Because I know how unreasonable, stubborn, un-caring, and narrow-minded he is!"

His grin faded with each of her words, and a look of curiosity replaced amusement. "Are you sure you have the right man in mind?"

She gazed beyond him in exasperation, trying to control her temper before she answered him. "Yes! And you're not winning any prizes, either! Here—" She reached into her purse for a twenty-dollar bill.

Suddenly his arms closed around her and he scooped her up against his broad chest. She yelped in shock, clutching her purse. Stunned at his audacity, then furious, she began to kick her feet and struggle to get free. He merely tightened his grip and strode toward her car.

"Put me down! I've got to see Brink Claiborn, and you're getting me dirty!"

"If you wanted to stay squeaky clean, you shouldn't have trespassed. You don't belong in a hard-hat area. If you want an appointment with Claiborn, call him. In the meantime you have to get out of here." He swung her on her feet beside her car and stretched out his arm to lean against the car, effectively blocking her path to the fenced area. He was physically commanding—overpowering, actually.

She raised her chin as if trying to overcome an enormous obstacle. Infuriated over his forcefulness, she stuffed the bills into her purse, then brushed dust off her dress. Finished, she gave him a glare, staring into implacable blue eyes that watched her calmly.

"I see he hires men to match his type of mentality! Brute force, rudeness. Just look at me! I'm as dusty as you are now!" She gave him another withering glare, but in response he merely followed her instructions to the letter.

Slowly, thoroughly, he studied her; it was another searing, all-consuming appraisal that slipped like warm fingers down her red dress, over her long legs, right down to her toes, a masculine assessment that made her pulse jump and heat rise in her cheeks. His mocking blue eyes finally clashed with her green ones.

"Want some help brushing off the dust?" he drawled in a husky voice that jangled her raw nerves in a uniquely disturbing manner.

"No!" She took a step backwards, noticed the twinkle in his eyes, and realized he had been teasing her. "You are without a doubt the most—"

"Most what?" he asked, leaning closer.

"Never mind!" She yanked open the door of her blue rental car and slipped inside, tossing her purse on the seat beside her. Seething with anger and with some other emotion she didn't care to recognize, she reached for the door handle.

He caught the door before she could slam it, stopping it instantly with the flex of powerful muscles. "Most what? Scared to say?"

"The second most infuriating man with whom I've ever had the misfortune to cross paths!"

"Me?" he asked with feigned innocence. "Infuriating to a lovely lady?"

Suddenly she was struck by his teasing expression, and she had to laugh.

When she did, his eyes sparkled and he leaned down so that his face was only inches from hers. "That's better," he said, making two simple words sensuous enough to raise the morning temperature a notch. "Look, call the office. What's your name? I'm sure Brink will talk to you," he added dryly. "I'll tell him to."

"He takes your advice?" she asked with obvious disbelief.

"Of course," he answered with amusement. "Aren't *you* going to take my advice?" His blue eyes had tiny silver flecks near the pupils; his brown lashes were thick and had a slight curl. His proximity made her pulse race again—a fact she didn't understand because it hadn't ever happened before in her life on first meeting with a man.

"Don't you think you should tell me your name and where you live?"

She was tempted—sorely tempted. He had adorable eyes and the sexiest body she had ever encountered; he could send her pulse skittering like pebbles under a spinning tire. . . .

But she didn't want to encourage him. He was brash enough with hostile discouragement! "There's no point. You can't talk your boss into seeing me."

"You don't know until you give it a try. I might be his right-hand man."

"Somehow I doubt it," she said condescendingly. "Now, if you'll close the car door, please . . ."

"You do smell sweet, like Obsession. And he will listen to me. Want to give me a phone number?"

Although Hilary was surprised that he could recognize her brand of perfume, she'd had enough of this disarming man. "Get out of my way," she said clearly.

With a wide grin he slowly straightened up, and she couldn't resist the incredible temptation to gaze down over firm musculature, a narrow waist, a flat stomach, and jeans that fit oh, so tightly!

Abruptly she looked up to see a mocking glint in his eyes as he stepped back and swung the door shut, giving her a nod that was a salute. He strode away, stepping over the wire barrier without breaking stride, his body moving with the ease of someone in excellent physical condition. Wind ruffled his wavy hair, and she couldn't take her eyes away from him. She had to admit there had been a chemistry between them that she hadn't ever experienced before.

He glanced over his shoulder, caught her watching, and waved, walking backward. She looked down

at her purse and the dusty smudge on her skirt.
Brushing vigorously, she tried to get her thoughts
back on Brink Claiborn, but it was difficult. When
she raised her head, the worker was talking to the
man in the suit. Both of them turned to look in her
direction and laughed.

Her temper exploded. All the frustration of the
past few days burst into red-hot fury over being
laughed at by the two men. The worker went back to
the building to kneel and study something at the
corner of the foundation. Brink Claiborn was still in
view.

He had moved farther away from the rubble and
was talking to someone. Hilary pounded the steering wheel with the palm of her hand. Tomorrow
morning she had to fly home. And Brink Claiborn
thought it was funny that he could effectively keep
her away from him!

Her aunts' cautions against acting impulsively evap-
orated to be replaced by bulldog determination. When
Hilary set her mind to something, she liked to see it
accomplished. She would see Mr. Brink Claiborn
now!

No longer acting with the benefit of cool logic, she
calculated swiftly. If she tried to walk across the
off-limits area, the worker would confront her again.
If she walked around the long way, he still could
spot her and prevent her from getting near his boss.
And she had no doubts he would do exactly that, if
only to break the monotony of his chores with a
little flirting.

She frowned and stared at the object of her dilemma. The brick wall blocked her approach from
the other two directions. Aggravation, as well as

frustration, mounted, a mental kaleidoscope playing in her mind of moments with her tearful aunts, the haughty receptionist at the Claiborn office, the rude housekeeper, the imperious secretary, and the muscle-bound, sexy worker who would run interference for his boss. She glared at the suited figure only three hundred yards away.

"Mr. Brink Claiborn, you're going to have to talk to me!" And a way to get him to do so came to her. It was a simple plan that wouldn't bother anyone except Mr. Claiborn, possibly—and he deserved to be disturbed!

Only a single strand of wire bordered the area. The ground was rough but relatively open, except for the building, small stones, broken bricks, glass, and a couple of piles of dirt. It was obvious from the packed dirt and the tracks that the men had driven their pickups, bulldozers, cars, and equipment over the lot many times. It would be so easy to drive only three hundred yards and confront her nemesis.

Hilary's pulse raced with determination while her gaze swept the area again. Vaguely she remembered past admonitions from her aunts to guard against her rash impulsiveness, but after all the discourteous refusals she had suffered because of Brink Claiborn, she forgot her aunts' warnings.

There was very little activity on the lot. Hilary suspected that they were getting ready to stop early for lunch because it was nearly noon, and most of the men seemed to be leaving. The only indication that she shouldn't be driving in the area was a small sign and a thin wire.

The fencing wire was held up by rusty green metal rods, a hasty barrier designed more to rope off the area than to keep people out. Of course, she would be trespassing, but that was only a minor infraction, and frustration was churning so hard within her that she simply couldn't fret about breaking a little law. The man in the suit looked directly her way, laughed, and then turned his back. Laughing at her, was he? How dare he!

It was the final straw!

Firming her lips and squaring her shoulders, she turned the ignition and glanced once more at the worker. He was still occupied with something on the ground, hunkered down, his faded, torn jeans pulling tightly on his long legs and narrow hips, his back momentarily to her.

Remembering how he and his boss had laughed at her, she felt her emotions inflame. She put the car in gear, pressed the gas pedal, and drove through the wire, hearing it hit the car and fall as the rods came out of the ground easily.

Men's heads snapped around to stare at her. Someone yelled; she glanced at the worker and saw him wave his arms and heard his shout. He started running, angling off between her and the object of her destination. She drove grimly, determined to get Brink Claiborn's attention no matter what.

She slanted a quick glance again and saw the worker running furiously; he was trying to intercept her. She pressed the gas pedal harder, and bounced over rocks, then had to hit the brakes when she noticed a shallow ditch ahead.

The car jolted, flying over the crevice. Her heart thudded when she saw that Brink Claiborn had finally given her his undivided attention, staring at her with fists on his hips, an expression of amazement on his pale face.

Looking to her left, she saw the workman running closer now, but a pile of rocks blocked his path. With startling swiftness he vaulted over the rocks, sailing above them, his booted feet gliding through the air for a moment that was etched in heart-stopping time. His legs bent slightly, and then he dropped to earth, landing like a cat on his feet and gaining his balance—directly in the path of her car!

Panic ripped through her as she slammed on her brakes, turning the wheel violently to swerve and miss him.

Her nerves were in shreds when the car finally rocked to a stop several yards to the left of him, dust spiraling up from the tires. The things some men did to make points with their employers! It had been idiotic for the man to leap into her path simply to keep the upper hand! He had endangered his life and shattered her composure with his rash action. Yanking open the car door, she stormed outside to tell him what she thought.

"You damn little fool!" he yelled, coming to meet her. "Get out of here!"

"I'm going to see—"

He caught her in his arms roughly this time, and her temper snapped as she fought him uselessly. He swung her down into the passenger seat of the car, then ran around the car and jumped in behind the wheel and threw the car in reverse.

She grabbed an ironlike wrist. "Get out of my car!"

Ignoring her, he twisted around, flung his arm over the back of the seat, and pressed down on the accelerator. The car lurched back so swiftly, it made her stop protesting and cling to the seat to keep from striking her head on the dashboard. His gaze was fierce as he steered the car toward the parking lot.

Finally, with a swirl of dust, the car spun around and skidded to a stop on the asphalt of the parking lot. He cut the ignition and turned to face her, his eyes blazing, his quiet voice cutting off the defiant words that rose to her lips.

"You little fool! We have sticks of dynamite placed all over that area. If you had hit one of them, you, this car, and any man near it could have been blown to smithereens!" He leaned closer, one arm draped over the steering wheel, the other across the back of his seat. "Don't you know what the words *caution* and *no trespassing* mean? A hard-hat area is dangerous!"

Stunned over his disclosure about the dynamite, her anger melted, and she stared at him, feeling as if she had shrunk to three inches in size.

He continued to glare at her, barely able to restrain his fury. Hilary was overcome with shame; she had jeopardized others and foolishly placed her life in danger. "I'm sorry," she said quietly, feeling a tremor start, an aftermath of emotional shock.

He was breathing heavily, glaring at her in silence, as if he were battling to control his emotions. "Call the office like a normal human being!" he growled, and flung himself out of the car.

He strode off, his shoulders square, no teasing wave over his shoulder this time. She trembled as her gaze raked the area and the men, still frozen, staring at her.

Embarrassed and shaken, Hilary gingerly put the car in gear and drove back to the hotel. There, she sought the refuge of her silent room with its solitary bed.

It took the better part of an hour for her nerves to calm. It took three hours before she worked up her courage to phone Claiborn Industries, Landfill and Compaction, and ask for Brink Claiborn.

This time she was put through to him immediately, and she sighed with relief while she waited for him to come on the line. In spite of the dangerousness, foolishness, and wrongness of her actions, her rash drive had pried him into confronting her. She felt a tiny bit better.

"Brink Claiborn," came a deep, businesslike voice.

"Mr. Claiborn, this is Hilary Wakefield from Natchez."

"The woman in the car," he said dryly, and she blushed with embarrassment.

"I'm sorry about that, but I desperately wanted to talk to you."

"Are you related to the Wakefield sisters?" he asked impassively.

"Yes. They're my aunts. I'd like to make an appointment to discuss the house, Saville, with you. I've flown all the way here from Mississippi to talk to you, and I won't take much of your time, but it's urgent."

"I've gone over the matter of the house with your aunts. They know my decision."

"Will you see me for just a few minutes?"

There was a long, silent pause. "I have a busy schedule—"

"I'm sure you do," she said, interrupting, bracing herself for rejection.

"A busy schedule," he repeated firmly, "more so at this time of year. It would be easier for me to talk over dinner."

She stared at the phone, feeling surprised and elated. Dinner would allow her more time than a brief meeting in his office! "That would be wonderful."

"Give me your address."

"I can meet you."

"Your address, please." The words were a command.

His cavalier manner elicited a mild spark of annoyance, but Hilary bit back a cutting response. "I'm at the Hilton on Bluegrass Drive."

"How's seven? We'll meet in the lobby."

"Excellent!"

"See you then, Hilary." The phone clicked and he was gone. The whole conversation hadn't lasted two minutes, but she felt her spirits lift. Dinner! That meant an hour to persuade him to listen to her aunts' proposal to let them buy his grandfather's old plantation home back in Natchez when it went on the market.

She glanced at her reflection in the mirror. She wanted to look her best tonight. Brink Claiborn was single and male—and she was determined to use those circumstances to her advantage.

A glance at her watch showed she had a few hours to shop. She had wanted to peruse the stores and salons ever since her arrival in Los Angeles, but her pursuit of Brink Claiborn had consumed all her time. Humming a tune, she picked up her purse and left the room, stepping into the bright California sunshine.

The hotel parking lot was bordered with tall palms and filled with shiny cars glinting in hot sunlight.

At the sight of her dusty car she remembered the blue-eyed workman, and her pulse did a ridiculous skip. Forget him, she told herself. She would never see him again. The next morning she would fly back to Mississippi, hopefully with her mission accomplished. As she hurried to her car, she had a recollection, as clear as the cloudless sky, of strong arms holding her. How had he known about Obsession? The answer came as swiftly as the question. He had been charismatic, sexy. His life was probably filled with women. She tried to shrug away thoughts about him as she drove down the boulevard in search of a dress to wear to dinner.

At ten minutes before seven she took one last look at herself, satisfied with the reflection of her soft yellow chiffon dress that clung to her waist, yet had a full skirt that flared when she walked. A high white collar and tiny pearl buttons down the front were dainty; her shoulders were bare where the bodice tapered to the collar. She wore dangling gold hoop earrings; her hair was swept back with tiny combs, so that soft curls fell across her back and above her shoulders. The few loose tendrils above her forehead were feathered away from her face.

Satisfied with her appearance, she picked up her small white evening bag and headed for the lobby, her heels clicking on the sidewalk until she turned the corner and entered a long, red-carpeted hallway that led to the spacious lobby.

Breathing deeply, satisfied that all was right in her world again, she surveyed lovely crystal chandeliers, white and green upholstered furniture, plush carpets, and masses of green plants.

She had deliberately arrived early so she could

watch for Brink Claiborn. The spotless glass doors showed an empty entranceway; her gaze traveled over the deserted lobby and swung to the desk where two uniformed clerks worked and a strikingly hand-some man leaned against the counter. The man's gaze met hers, and she stopped dead in her tracks.

Two

He wore a flawlessly tailored charcoal suit, a conservative blue tie, and a white shirt with gold links showing at the cuffs. The white stood out against his deeply tanned skin; the suit emphasized his broad shoulders and narrow hips. The tie was the shade of his eyes, highlighting their crystal-blue color. Hilary felt as if her lungs had ceased to function, her heart had stopped pumping, and her brain had gone on hold. Shock riveted her to the spot as he casually moved away from the counter. His gaze scrutinized her more thoroughly than she had assessed him, yet a faint smile softened his intense stare.

As he approached in an easy walk, she took a deep breath. Her heart started pounding, and her brain jumped from one thought to another with the swiftness of lightning. Emotions tore at her. Shock, surprise, anger, and a strong current of exhilaration raged within her. But anger dominated.

"Why didn't you tell me?" she asked when he paused a few steps away.

He shrugged. "I sure tried to, but you wouldn't listen. I told you I was Brink Claiborn, remember? You need to learn a lesson about making snap assumptions about people," he said, but there was no real bite in his accusation.

She was beautiful; his pulse hummed as he watched her, and he wanted to reach out and touch her. Electricity. The reactions he experienced around Hilary Wakefield were more volatile than the dynamite he handled at work. In spite of her foolishness today, he admired her for taking matters into her own hands, and he admired her determination, two qualities he understood well.

"The man in the suit looked as if he were giving orders to everyone, even to you. Who was he?"

"An engineer who works for me. He was explaining how to set off the charges. I may be president of the company, but I take the advice of my experts. Just because I was dressed in dusty jeans and he wore a suit, you automatically figured he was the boss and I was the not-too-bright employee," he said, teasing her to see what kind of reaction he could get.

"I didn't say you weren't too bright! I didn't imply it, either!" she responded firmly.

"You tried to bribe me," he said, breathing in deeply as he detected a trace of her enticing perfume. Why did she have to be a Wakefield? The Wakefield sisters had driven him to desperate measures with their incessant phone calls, interminable conversations, unreasonable demands, and hopeless proposals. And here was another generation of Wakefield who reworked his pulse and clogged his thought processes with just a swish of her hips or a green-eyed glance. "And as I recall upon our first crossing paths," he added, "you told me that Brink Claiborn was 'stubborn, uncaring, narrow-minded—' "

"I remember!" she snapped, flushing with embarrassment. His brows arched, his eyes gave her a merry serves-you-right twinkle, and she had to smile in return.

"Ah, that's better."

"For such a stubborn, uncaring, narrow-minded man, you do have another side that's all charm."

"That's a lot better," he said softly, moving a step closer and letting his voice drop to a sensuous level. "I'm sorry if you had a bad time at my office with my receptionist, but she was only following orders. And I had no idea my secretary would tell you I had gone to Europe. I guess I was a little too emphatic in saying I didn't want to talk to a Wakefield."

"I know. You wanted to avoid me at all costs," she said lightly, feeling a giddy merriment replacing the tattered shreds of impatience and anger.

"Well, about that, I'll have to admit to a giant degree of dim-wittedness!"

She laughed, he smiled, and Hilary felt a warmth that had nothing to do with the temperature in the quiet lobby, which was pleasantly air-conditioned.

"Shall we start over? I'm glad to meet you, Hilary Wakefield," he said in a voice that conveyed his intrigue and curiosity. He held out his hand.

When she felt his big fingers wrap around her slender ones, Hilary remembered how it had felt to be held in his arms, pressed hard against his heart. *Charismatic* wasn't a strong enough word for the appeal that oozed from every pore of Mr. Brink Claiborn's body!

"And I'm glad to meet you officially, Brink Claiborn. I've waited a long, long time," she added softly, knowing she was flirting with danger. The man must be a heartbreaker, and she didn't want to board the plane the next day with a shattered heart.

"As for putting you off, I'll try to make it up to you. If I'd only known, you wouldn't have had to wait fifteen seconds to talk to me!" he said, his fingers still holding hers, his thumb moving leisurely back and forth across her tiny wrist, making her incredibly aware of his touch.

"Do you suppose people will wonder why we're standing here in the lobby so long, shaking hands forever?"

His eyes sparkled as he winked at her. "Let's go," he said, taking her arm. She tried to match her steps to his long stride, aware of the brush of their shoulders, his suit coat touching her arm, his fingers laced in hers. "Why were you using dynamite today? In your line of work, I thought you filled in holes in the earth, not made them."

"Usually that's true, but the Delmar people have built a new plant, and they want the ruins of the old factory out of their way so they can use the dirt for bricks. They told me about their plans, and I agreed to demolish the old structure. Occasionally I get into odd jobs. In this business, all sorts of things crop up." While he talked, he stretched out his arm and held open the glass door for her, then escorted her across the parking lot to a shiny black Lincoln.

He seated her in the car, and she watched him walk around to the driver's side, still amazed at the discovery of his identity. Amazed and delighted, she had to admit. And yet, she also had to face the realization that she probably wouldn't see him after tonight.

He started the car. "This will be a better ride than last time," he said, smiling at her.

"Don't bring it up, please. I was so embarrassed. I didn't mean to endanger anyone, including myself!"

"I didn't mean to snap at you," he said as they turned into a lane of traffic.

"Oh really?" she chided gently. "You'd yell at me again if I repeated that performance!"

At the corner he turned off the busy four-lane highway onto a quiet residential street and slowed at the curb near a row of small A-frame houses. She had just begun to wonder what he was doing when he cut the motor and faced her. One of his arms stretched out behind her on the back of the seat and his other hand reached out to brush her collar, the touch intensifying her awareness of him. "I can't drive one block farther without apologizing for shouting at you. I lost my cool because it was a wonder you didn't trigger the explosion of at least one stick of dynamite. As it was, you ran over one, and it didn't go off."

She stared at him, lost in a gaze that was steadfast and compelling, stunned more by the pull on her senses than the fact that she had been in such danger earlier. "Apology accepted. You didn't need to pull over and park to tell me. I deserved to be shouted at."

He shook his head and caught a lock of her hair to twine it around his callused finger, watching her while he did. Brink couldn't believe the effect she was having on him; he hadn't felt this strongly about a woman since he was about fifteen years old—and that hardly counted. He remembered how amused he had been earlier in the day at her description of him, and then how horrified he had been when she had driven through the wire barrier. She had scared him senseless and enraged him, but once he had calmed down, he blamed himself. He should have convinced her who he was in the first place, sparing her that wild, dangerous ride.

Now she was watching him with a languorous, sensuous look that set him on fire. He'd been a fool, refusing to talk to her or to see her. Now he thanked his good fortune that he had been given another chance.

Remembering how she had felt in his arms, he took a deep breath and wished he could pull her close to him. It was ridiculous, yet as compelling as the moon on the tides. He had known enough women that his blood shouldn't boil at the mere proximity of this particular woman, but it did. Oh, how it did! As Brink ran his finger along her jaw, he noticed the flicker in her eyes, the slight parting of her lips. She was as drawn as he!

And yet Brink had to remind himself that she was a Wakefield. Maybe she was working on him deliberately, pretending to be charmed because it was to her benefit. He was treading on dangerous ground with a Wakefield. Her aunts were nuisances of the highest order. Yet as swiftly as caution came, he dismissed it. When she hadn't known who he was, she had been as attracted to him as now.

He wanted to kiss her. He leaned closer, so close that he could feel her breath against his skin, and she tilted her head up. "Maybe I'm glad I didn't take your first call," he said softly.

It took a few seconds for her to focus on him, and his pulse raced when he realized how dazzled she had been by the prospect of their kiss. Suddenly he wanted it to be very special—a kiss she'd always remember. He had a growing suspicion it would be a moment he wouldn't forget—ever.

"Why?" she asked in a soft, breathless voice. "Maybe it would have solved everything weeks ago."

"And we might have finished our discussion on the phone, before I had a chance to meet you. And I would have missed today. It's been the most interesting day of my life."

She laughed then, a silvery bit of laughter that broke the tension between them and made him smile in return.

"I guess I lost my last shred of patience when I saw you and your engineer laughing at me."

"What are you talking about?"

"After you left me, you went over to him, and I presumed you told him about me."

"We were talking about something that happened this morning. I wasn't laughing at you, even if it looked that way." Another ten seconds and he would be reaching for her, holding her. . . . With an effort he turned to the wheel. "Shall we go to dinner?"

"Sure," she answered. "And I know it couldn't have been the most interesting day of your life!"

"It just might have been. It isn't over yet, you know," he drawled, lowering his voice to an intimate tone.

He saw the quick rise of her breasts as she inhaled and held her breath, the faint narrowing of her eyes. Her breasts swelled against the fabric of her dress, and he mentally undressed her, aching to unfasten every one of those damn pearl buttons. He couldn't remember having such an immediate, earth-shaking reaction to a woman, and he intended to draw out the moment. He wanted her to be on fire with longing when he kissed her, because he suspected his system would be a raging inferno.

"We have a long evening ahead," he said, letting his feelings change the texture of his voice, relishing her response. His body reacted, too, a swift stirring that jolted his senses.

He started the motor and headed back to the highway, wishing now that he had told her they would have dinner at his place.

"How come we're both from Natchez and we've never met?" he asked, driving with his elbow propped on the open window.

She shrugged. "I suppose because we're not the same age. I'm twenty-seven—"

"And I'm thirty-three," he added.

"See? We wouldn't have been in school at the same time. The population is over twenty-four thousand, big enough that everyone doesn't know everyone else."

"Our relatives know each other."

"They've had more years and more opportunities. And a reason to get to know each other. Besides, I've heard about you, and you've heard about me. After all, both our families lived at Saville at one time or another."

"I hadn't heard how pretty you are."

"Thank you."

"Do you live in Natchez now?"

"Yes. I have an antique shop," she answered, amused that he had neatly avoided pursuing why her relatives had a reason to know his. "My father passed away when I was finishing school. After college, while I was floundering around trying to find work and caring for my sick mother, the opportunity arose to buy the place. The shop had been in business over fifteen years, and it seemed like a good investment. When Mother died, I took my inheritance and used part of it to purchase the shop."

"I'm sorry about your folks. That's rough—especially to lose them so close together. My parents are gone too. There's only Granddad, and you know how bad his health is."

"I heard that he had another stroke recently."

"Yeah, the nursing home called me, but they said it wasn't severe and not to fly home just because of it. I was busy, so I didn't."

He turned into a lot, parked, and entered a restaurant decorated with pink flamingos and lime carpeting with white wicker furniture and linen-covered tables. A man played and sang in the bar, the piano music carrying into the main dining room and to their table, in a secluded corner behind a grouping of greenery.

It took a great deal of effort for Hilary to concentrate on the large green menus because her attention was captured by Brink. Over glasses of chilled Chenin Blanc he said, "I've probably been in your antique shop. I usually browse through them when I'm home."

"We've gotten in some particularly pretty pieces

lately. We're getting ready for the Pilgrimage. The crowds seem to grow each year," she said, thinking momentarily about Natchez's big event, when some of the lovely old homes were opened for tours.

"Do you live with your aunts?"

"Heavens, no!" she answered with a laugh, and noticed how the reflection of the candlelight highlighted his wide cheekbones.

"Why the violent reaction?" he asked, taking her hand in his and turning it. "There's no ring. Is there a steady man in your life?"

"Heavens, no!" she repeated, not quite as vehemently.

"What a relief—if it's the truth!"

"Of course I'm telling you the truth," she said, flirting with him.

"There's no steady woman in my life."

"I didn't ask."

"I know you didn't," he chided playfully, and her pulse hummed with pleasure. He still held her hand, releasing it only when the crystal plates with green salad arrived.

She studied his attractive features, set off by straight brows. He had combed his thick, wavy brown hair, yet it was just as attractive now as it had been earlier at the Delmar plant when it had been tangled by the wind. At last she asked, "How'd you get so far from home?"

"I played football on a college scholarship in California, and then just stayed on to work here. I had construction jobs and one summer did demolition, then got a chance to buy this small company. It's grown while I've had it, and the work is interesting.

Besides, I'm not cooped up in an office much of the time."

"No, I can see that!" She paused while steaming plates with broiled lobster tails, melted butter, and snow peas on wild rice were placed before them. While they ate, she asked, "Do you get home often?"

"No." He paused, still holding a bite of flaky white lobster on the end of his fork, ready to dip into golden butter. Lowering his fork to his plate, he gave her one of his scorching looks, which made her appetite disappear. "But I will more often now."

"Shall we discuss the reason we're having dinner together?"

"Gladly," he answered, a faint smile deepening the creases in his cheeks. "I couldn't wait to see you again."

The ripple of pleasure that coursed through her in the wake of his statement didn't stop her from shaking her head in protest. "That's not why we're together now, and you know it! We need to discuss Saville. My aunts—"

"Why don't we discuss business after dinner? We can go to my place."

Every shred of common sense she possessed told her to be firm with him and insist on discussing the future of Saville right now. A faint, coaxing smile tugged at his features, making crinkles appear at his eyes, and she couldn't resist. She sighed and smiled in return. "It's a crime . . ."

"What is?"

"Your charm!"

Brink felt a flush of pleasure. He knew she was teasing, merely flirting with him, but her answer tickled his senses. He winked at her. "Had enough?"

"What? Food or your charm?"

"You can have any dessert on the menu, or we can get up and go where we can be alone and discuss Saville, and I can offer you an after-dinner drink or lemonade or a bowl of ice cream."

"How can I resist that offer?"

They both smiled before he turned to catch the waiter's attention and ask for the check.

"Is anything wrong with dinner, sir?"

"The dinner was excellent," Brink said at the same time Hilary remarked, "It was wonderful!"

Satisfied, the waiter glanced at Hilary and left to get their check.

"We insulted him by leaving so much uneaten," Hilary said.

"Don't be ridiculous. I saw the look he gave you. He knows why I want to leave now." He paid the check that was placed at his elbow, and within minutes they were on the way to his house.

"Where do you live?" he asked as they sped along the freeway.

"In a duplex. It's on a bluff overlooking the river."

"Somehow I pictured you living in a house like Saville."

"Not me, thank you!"

"You're in the antique business. You must appreciate old things."

"I do appreciate them, and I know them well. I grew up with them."

"So you don't want them around all the time now?"

"That's right," she said. He shook his head, and she sensed his disapproval.

"You don't agree?"

He shrugged. "I love old things. I go home every

year or so and make the Pilgrimage just like a tourist. Each mansion is a special treasure, filled with beauty and ties to a past that was an important part of America's history."

"You sound like a tour guide!"

He frowned and glanced at her, then smiled. "And you sound like Miss Hilary Modern."

Three

They entered Brink's house through sliding glass doors in the rear, where a terrace overlooked a well-manicured lawn. The kitchen they entered was spacious and modern.

"And you're the one who says he loves old houses!" Hilary declared.

"This place is comfortable," he said, watching her as he tossed the car keys onto a white counter. He slipped off his coat and loosened his tie without taking his gaze from hers. Suddenly the volatile attraction that could flare so easily between them ignited, tugging at her senses and taking her breath.

"Never again will I refuse to see someone the first time she asks," he said softly, the words an invisible caress.

"And I won't ever drive over dynamite again," she whispered.

He moved closer, and with each step her pulse quickened. He was incredibly handsome, a blatantly sexy man, physically powerful. She knew her heart was in grave danger as his fingers brushed a lock of hair away from her shoulder.

Aching to kiss her, Brink watched her intently. He wanted to kiss her, passionately and thoroughly, so that she wouldn't forget him when she got on the plane back to Mississippi, because he had a suspicion that he would never forget her! He slid his thumb to her collarbone, relishing the feel of her silky, smooth skin.

"Hilary," he said, letting his breath fan out as he exhaled deeply. He was caught in her spell, trembling with need. She tilted her face back slightly, her mouth turning up to him, her tongue running across her full lower lip. He groaned, slipping his arms around her, unable to wait a second longer. He leaned forward, trying to exercise control, trying to make the moment last because it was exquisite torment. His lips brushed her cheek, searching for her voluptuous mouth.

When she moaned softly and swayed toward him, he conquered her lips, lost to an unbearable need. His mouth moved to cover hers, his lips opening hers, his tongue sliding hotly into her mouth as he pulled her hard against him.

Hilary yielded to his kisses like a burning desert flower opening itself to rain. Compelled by a fervent desire, she basked in his embrace until finally, breathlessly, she leaned back.

"We need to discuss Saville," she said, smoothing his collar, letting her hand drift down on his chest. "What will I tell my aunts when I arrive at their doorstep tomorrow? That Brink Claiborn chastised me, took me to dinner, then kissed me?"

"What am I going to have to do to make you forget that I lost my temper today?"

Hilary's emotions were spinning in a giddy spiral that she had never experienced before. She usually didn't flirt, she wasn't forward with men, but something about Brink brought out reactions that were as fierce as they were playful.

"After those kisses, I can just barely remember," she said, expecting an equally teasing rejoinder.

Instead, his eyes darkened and his arms tightened around her. "Good. Another kiss or two and the memory might fade completely." And then all her thoughts faded as he kissed her hard, his arms crushing the breath from her lungs.

This woman set Brink on fire. Her kisses were burning flames that danced over him, branding him deep inside. He barely knew her, yet he couldn't remember life without her. He caressed her, weaving his hands through her hair. Although he knew that some women hated to have their hair mussed, he was certain that Hilary didn't care. She was sensual, responsive to his every touch. This was a woman who belonged in a man's bed, a woman made for loving. The realization caused him to shake with need. Startled by the depth of his reaction, he released her abruptly and strode to the glass doors to open the latch.

"Come sit outside. I'll get drinks. I'm a whiz at Irish coffee."

She already felt heady—just from his kisses! "I'd better keep a clear head. But I'll take a glass of water."

He smiled at her, casually leaning against the door. "Do you always have this effect on men?"

Her heart thumped violently as she wondered if he shared her giddy excitement. "No, but I suspect you always have this effect on women."

"Let's go outside and see if our friendship can weather our disagreement."

"Our friendship? We barely know each other." She smiled as she crossed the room.

"But we *do* know each other. We've had unforgettable moments together."

"That's true," she replied as she followed him outside. "But friends are close and can depend on each other."

"You can depend on me," he said, pulling a pale yellow garden chair up to face hers as she sat down. She gazed out over the breathtaking view. The lawn stretched out to a beach where waves crashed ashore and receded in a steady rhythm.

"This is beautiful!" she exclaimed. "I love my view of the river, but this is glorious!"

"Yeah, after the work I do all day, this is nice and relaxing." He leaned back, propping one ankle on his knee, locking his fingers behind his head. "I love the old houses of the South, but I can't live there permanently because I have a sizable business here. When I inherit, I want Saville turned into a museum."

Here it comes, she thought, the end of a promising friendship, the end of an attraction more explosive than the dynamite on the construction site. Hilary took a deep breath and looked him squarely in the eye.

"Aunt Sophie and Aunt Mavis and my father were born in that house. Their parents, the Wakefields, owned Saville until Grandpa Wakefield's business failed. Daddy was the youngest when they lost it. He was only five, but Mavis was eleven and Sophie was thirteen. They spent their childhood in that house, and they love it as much as they love each other."

"I don't blame them. I love that old house too."

Lucky house, she thought briefly.

"I grew up there, remember? Dad died when I was four, and Mom went home to live with Granddad and my grandmother."

"Since you have legal control of your grandfather's financial affairs, my aunts sent me here to plead their case. All they want to do is live the rest of their lives at Saville. They'll pay whatever you ask; you won't have to come down a penny on the price."

"I don't intend to," he said dryly.

"And they'll agree to a provision in their wills that it be sold for a museum. You'll have what you want, and they'll have what they want."

"No."

She felt a flare of annoyance as his abrupt answer reminded her of all those times she had run up against his stubborn will. "There you go again."

"Doing what? Refusing your request?"

"Being stubborn. Let's discuss the matter."

"Sure, discuss away." He hooked a chair with his toe and dragged it closer to prop his feet on it. When he stretched out his long legs, it became an effort for her to keep her gaze from sliding down the length of him.

"You don't stand to lose anything," she insisted. When he rolled his eyes, she snapped, "You don't! What would you lose?"

"Time. The house would weather and age without the proper care."

"But if you sell the house to Aunt Sophie and

Aunt Mavis, you would have two women living in it who care for it very much!"

He put his feet on the ground and scooted closer to her. "What do you do in Natchez for fun?"

"Don't change the subject. We're not through."

He ran his finger along her bare arm, tantalizing her. "I'm not changing the subject. I'm just wondering about you. What do you do for fun?"

"I date; we go to New Orleans sometimes, or we go to a show, or we sit at home and watch a movie on the VCR, or we have dinner on a boat on the river—very simple pleasures."

Brink felt a strange twinge of envy. He didn't want to think about Hilary going out with anyone else, and the realization shocked him. He usually was very casual in his approach to his women friends. They were friends, sometimes lovers, but he could always walk away without looking back. Why did he dread the moment when he would say good-bye to Hilary?

"New Orleans. Would you go to New Orleans with me sometime?"

She laughed merrily, and the sound jangled his nerves. "Sure, Brink. Call whenever you want to go! But it will have to be next week or the week after. I'll be too busy when the Pilgrimage starts."

"Don't laugh. I come home sometimes," he said, narrowing his eyes to study her. Her skin was flawless and smooth, her cheeks rosy. Her mouth was full and well shaped, and every time he looked at her lips, he wanted to lean forward and brush them with his own. "What do you like to do in New Orleans?"

"Go to Preservation Hall. I don't care if I have to

stand for hours jammed into a one-foot space, I love the music."

"Dixieland jazz. What else do you like?"

"To see Aunt Sophie and Aunt Mavis happy. You have a real knack for changing the subject."

He shrugged. "I just want to know more about you. I already know about the house and your aunts."

"Stop being evasive. They adore the house. How can you prefer to see it made into a dusty old museum rather than enjoyed by two people who cherish it?"

"A museum can be enjoyed by thousands of visitors and the house will be preserved for posterity."

"You can do that after Aunt Sophie and Aunt Mavis have lived in it. They're in their sixties—"

"And if they're half as healthy as Granddad, who'll be ninety-two this year, then they'll live in the house so long that it will be a ruin before I see it turned into a museum. By that time *I'll* probably be sixty years old!"

"That's ridiculous!"

"It isn't. I told you, I'm thirty—"

"That isn't what I meant. It's ridiculous to think that Saville would deteriorate in that time. The house is almost a hundred and fifty years old now, and it's in good shape."

"That's because my family took care of it."

Suddenly aggravated, she leaned forward with her elbows on her knees. "Why are you being so cold-hearted?"

He pushed his chair away and went to stand at the edge of the terrace, jamming his hands into his pockets and making his charcoal trousers stretch tautly across his hips.

"Not coldhearted—practical."

"Why can't you face me and say that?"

He turned around and strode purposefully across the terrace. Hauling her to her feet with his hands on her arms, he growled, "Because when I look into your big, green eyes, I want to give you anything you ask. My brain gets scrambled."

"I find that difficult to believe when you're as adamant as ever!" she snapped, her heartbeat skipping dangerously. He was compelling and dynamic, a powerful man who could charm the birds out of the trees. To fight him was more than difficult; it was next to impossible.

"I've listened to your arguments, but you haven't heard all of mine," she added, thinking his brain couldn't be more scrambled than hers was at the moment.

"Go ahead. I'll listen."

But the words died on her lips. She knew she should stick to business, but whenever she came close to him, something strange happened. It was like stepping into a magnetized field; the attraction was impossible to see, yet the force of it was overwhelming.

He drew a sharp breath, and his eyes narrowed as he gazed at her lips. "Want to kiss, or talk?"

Startled, she blinked and tried to step back while her face flushed with embarrassment and anger. He watched her closely. "You want to kiss," he said softly. "I can see it in your eyes . . . I can read it on your lips."

"You do too," she answered, then pulled away from him. "But we're going to talk," she said firmly, trying to convince herself. She sank back in the chair, and he sat across from her again.

"You'll get your museum with Aunt Mavis and Aunt Sophie, just later, that's all."

"They could change their minds about that ten seconds after signing the contract for the house! Even if they would keep their promise, I don't want to wait. To tell you the truth, your aunts probably can't keep up with the maintenance on a house that size. Look at where they live now."

"They live in a lovely old home. It just isn't as large or as fine or as old as Saville."

"No, but that isn't what I mean. They—" He stopped when a loud knock came on the high wooden fence on the east side of the house.

Four

"Hi, Brink. I was late getting in and saw your car. I thought maybe you'd want to grill—" The dark-haired woman who'd entered through a gate in the fence broke off as she spotted Hilary. "I'm sorry. You said you'd be alone tonight."

"My plans changed," he said easily. "Come meet someone from my hometown. Hilary, this is my next-door neighbor, Kiki Jensen. Kiki, this is Hilary Wakefield."

Kiki Jensen seemed startled when Brink said Hilary's name. "One of the Wakefields of Natchez?"

"Yes, I'm a Wakefield. You've heard about my aunts?" Hilary asked sweetly.

"Sure," Kiki said, flouncing down on a chair. "Now I understand the connection. I was thinking of the older women when he first said Wakefield."

"I'm here on their behalf."

"Are you making a dent in Brink's refusal to sell?"

"No, not so far," Hilary said lightly, hoping her

voice sounded normal. Kiki acted as if she were at home here, casually running her fingers along Brink's arm when he sat down nearby.

Hilary felt a pang of anxiety as she realized that Brink and she were worlds apart. He was a charmer, and he had a beautiful, friendly next-door neighbor.

"But it's not over yet," Brink chided gently. "I'm still discussing the matter with you. Right?"

"Of course," she said, smiling at him. He winked at her, and suddenly she felt better.

"Did you just get to town?" Kiki asked.

"I got in yesterday. It's taken me this long to get to see him," Hilary answered with good-natured humor.

"You won't ever be kept waiting again," Brink added in a voice that conveyed an absolute promise.

Hilary realized they were shutting Kiki out of the conversation and turned to ask politely, "Is this your hometown?"

"Oh, no. I'm from Akron. I came out here because I want to be a singer," she said.

The phone rang, and Brink stood up. "I'll be right back," he said as he strode into the house.

Hilary smiled at Kiki. "Have you succeeded with your singing?"

"Not yet. I'm still a receptionist more than a singer." Kiki glanced at the door, then rose. "Look, I know I'm intruding. Tell Brink I'll see him later."

"Don't go! You're not interrupting anything. Really. I came to L.A. to talk to him about selling the house to my aunts."

Kiki shook her head. "I'm intruding, whether you know it or not. I've never seen Brink so . . . captivated. He doesn't usually give women his full attention. I just want you to know that there's nothing between him and me except that we're good friends and good neighbors."

Hilary laughed before saying, "You don't need to explain that to me, and you don't need to go, either."

"I need to do both. You see, I've known Brink two years now, and I've never known him to act this way around any other woman."

"I just met him."

"Serves him right, then. He can be a real heart-breaker." She tilted her head to one side. "Maybe this once he's met his match."

"Not in me!"

Kiki smiled. "Keep up the good work. I love him, but he deserves to find out how it feels." She crossed the terrace quickly and waved before she stepped through the gate.

Hilary settled back in her chair, glancing at the open glass door and wondering about Kiki's strange confidences. She shook her head. Brink was a heart-breaker, all right. She had guessed that earlier that day, but the idea that he was captivated by her was absurd.

A slight breeze came off the water, tugging at her hair. How different his life was from hers in Natchez. When she heard Brink's footsteps, she turned to face him.

"Where's Kiki?"

"She said she had to go."

He dropped down in his chair and took her hand. "Where were we?"

"Discussing a house. You have a gorgeous home that is modern and functional and attractive, enjoyed by you and your friends. What do you care about the old house in Natchez? You won't even be there!"

He sat back and stared at her. "A museum will be protected and preserved. As I said before, hundreds of people can enjoy it."

"Only superficially. They'll appreciate it when they walk through it, and that's all."

"That's a lot. It's history; it deserves to be preserved."

"You sound as if my aunts are going to chop it up for firewood!"

"There you go, letting that temper of yours flare."

"I don't have a temper!"

"Whoo! What was that today when you practically ran me down? Do you know you missed me by only feet?"

"That's because you jumped right in front of my car! You scared me to pieces! And I understand now why you did." She glared at him. "Maybe you should take me back to the hotel!"

Suddenly he leaned forward, his hands closing on the arms of her chair, his knees touching her, imprisoning her in the chair. His voice dropped to a husky note. "No way are we going to part fighting."

"That's what you think!" she snapped, but some of the force had gone out of her voice. "You don't care about people!" she exclaimed. "You're interested in a museum that's devoid of life. I wouldn't have taken off work and flown out here to see you if— "

"So you're not glad you came?"

"You keep the charm going all the time, don't you?"

"Only with you." His face was only inches away, his gaze flicking from her eyes to her mouth and back. "I mean it. Hilary Wakefield, of the troublesome Natchez Wakefields, you're damn special."

"Sure." She forced herself to look away. "But you won't see me after tonight—unless you come back to Natchez."

"Do you really think I'll let you walk out of my life?"

"Frankly, yes. We can't seem to agree on anything."

"On a house," he whispered. "But we agree on this absolutely." He leaned closer, tilting his head so he could kiss her.

"Brink . . ." Her words dissolved the moment his lips touched hers, and magic exploded in a tempestuous flame that scorched like a desert sun. His arms slipped around her waist, and hers around his neck, and in seconds he moved her to his lap to hold her close. Even as he kissed away her fear and aggravation, he fueled a white-hot fire within her.

She wound her fingers in his soft hair, letting them drift down over his shoulders, rippling with muscles that were as hard as rocks. His hand trailed down her side and over her hipbone, lightly touching her thigh.

"Brink," she protested softly, easing herself off his lap. Although it was dark, she could see his expression; her breath caught at the hungry intensity in his eyes. No man had ever looked at her with such obvious and overwhelming desire.

"We'd better stop. I haven't said all I want to say to you."

He ran his fingers through his hair in a worried gesture and stood up to walk away. "I'll get us a drink."

In moments he returned with two tall glasses of lemonade, and they sat quietly watching stars twinkle in the velvety sky.

"Want to walk down to the beach? There's a path, and I'm sure we can find our way in the moonlight."

"Brink, this is fun, but I've flown all the way across the United States to talk to you about Saville. Please think about my aunts' offer. They will probably pay more than your asking price just to get the house."

"Hilary," he said, hating to have to refuse her, "your aunts can't take care of the small house they're living in now. I've visited them at home, and I've seen the place."

"Their home is beautiful!"

"Go look again," he said gently. "The flowers are pretty, their antiques are lovely, but the house is falling apart."

"That isn't so!"

"You're so accustomed to their house that I'd wager you don't really notice the problems."

Her eyes narrowed. "I've known a few people who won't let anyone wear shoes in their houses or walk on the carpets or sit on living-room furniture. You prefer me and everyone else who comes to see you to stay outside. I might get a footprint on your carpet, a smudge on your wall. I'll bet you're—"

He shoved back his chair swiftly, scooped her up into his arms, and strode inside.

"What are you doing? You have an arrogant side to you that just beats all—"

He flung her on the sofa, and she bounced, twisting and scrambling to regain her balance. "I've had it with your stubborn ways!" she protested.

He flipped on the light switches, revealing a room furnished in deep shades of blue with leather upholstery, blue carpet, and pale blue drapes. "You can walk all over this house. You can stand on my sofa if you want, sit wherever you want," he said. "My furniture is meant to be lived with, but it's also durable. I take care of it and my house in a reasonable manner. Your aunts don't!"

She glared at him. "Why don't you take me back to my hotel?"

"Why do you make me lose all control?" he asked, his tone suddenly soft.

"You aren't behaving normally?" she asked, moving to the kitchen and picking up her purse.

He shook his head. "Hardly. You bring out all sorts of violent reactions in me."

"I can't argue with that! Shall we go?"

He crossed the room, took hold of her purse, and pulled gently. She released it, and he placed it on the kitchen counter. He laced his fingers in hers. "Come here . . . please," he said in a coaxing tone. "We can't let the evening end this way."

"Brink, we can't agree, so why argue further?"

"I wasn't going to argue. Come on, just stay for a few minutes."

Still anxious to make a plea for Saville, she nodded and followed him outside. He led the way to the beach. Her fingers linked through his, she followed the narrow path that resembled a gray ribbon in the moonlight.

On the beach, they wandered down to the water's edge, letting the cool breeze blow over them as they faced the water. She turned to find him watching her.

"I shouldn't have picked you up. I'm not usually given to actions like that, but you do bring out something in me that others don't."

"Violence?"

"Not beyond picking you up when you need it. I guess I'm a little hotheaded. Sorry."

"Apology accepted."

"And will you do what I asked?"

"What?"

"When you're home, take a good long look at your aunts' house."

"I will, but I like that place so much, I know I've looked many times. When the azaleas bloom, they have one of the prettiest yards in town."

"I know they do, but it's because of the flowers. Enough said for now. Let's enjoy the moonlight and the ocean." He took her hand. "Those high heels weren't meant for sand."

"No," she said, slipping them off, aware of his hands steadying her as she balanced on first one foot and then the other. She looked up at him, and suddenly he hugged her, then draped his arm across her shoulders.

They strolled and chatted amicably. She watched him skip rocks, seeing the splashes in the silvery moonlight. At last, reluctantly, they returned to the hotel where he rode the elevator up with her and walked her to her door. "Am I coming in to see your room?"

She laughed and shook her head. "Nice try! No, sorry, but it's been fun, except for the matter of business between us. Brink, think about it a little more. Think about people instead of just a shell of a house. Think of a home that holds memories for two sweet ladies."

"You're sweet, Hilary," he said softly, moving closer, slipping his hands around her waist. "It's been unforgettable. Let me pick you up for breakfast and take you to the airport."

"Don't you have to go to work?"

"They can carry on for a few hours without me," he said dryly, teasing her, before he leaned slowly down to kiss her.

Moments later, she felt dazed as she told him good night and entered her room. " 'Night, Brink," she repeated before she closed the door.

" 'Night, Hilary," he said, walking backward, watching her.

"Brink!"

He bumped into a palm tree, steadied it, and smiled at her, waving as he went down the hall. She leaned out to watch him, for a moment remembering the sight of him in tight jeans and tattered T-shirt. Finally she closed the door, leaning against it and smiling dreamily until she thought of going home the next day, telling Brink good-bye, and facing her aunts with the news of his stubborn refusal to sell Saville.

Brink was waiting for her in the lobby, and her pulse jumped at the sight of him. Dressed in dark slacks, a white shirt, and a maroon tie, he looked extraordinarily handsome, and as she walked toward him, she became conscious of herself, of her new pale blue denim skirt and blue chambray shirt. Her hair was tied loosely behind her head with a blue ribbon.

"Wow! What a way to start my day!" he said softly, causing another flurry in her pulse.

"I think so too," she said, impulsively standing on tiptoe and kissing his cheek.

"Sure you wouldn't like to cancel your flight and

stay over the weekend?" he asked, slipping his arm around her waist. "You could be my guest."

"Thanks," she answered warmly, "but I have to get back to the shop."

They stepped out into sunshine, crossing the lot to his car while they argued about her staying over, but she was firm. And deep down she wondered if she was a little afraid of this man. She had a very peaceful life and he was a heartbreaker! Kiki's comments had confirmed Hilary's suspicions about him.

As soon as they were on the highway, she said, "I'll see my aunts in hours. Did you have any second thoughts?"

"Second, third, fourth, into the hundreds, all about you," he said softly, winking at her. "This is a nice way to start the day."

"To think I couldn't even get you to talk to me on the telephone! Suppose you're making as big a mistake about the house?"

"That's entirely different. I thought you were your aunts calling me, and I had already talked to them hour upon hour, endless times. You have some things going for you that make your persistence the grandest thing that's ever happened to me."

She shook her head at him. "If I'm a persistent pest, you're stubborn, charming, and impossible! And you won't listen to reason."

"Sure I will. We'll talk about it over orange juice. What did you take in college?"

"There you go hopping to another subject to evade the issue."

"Nope. I want to know all about you."

"I was an art major at the University of Mississippi."

"Do you paint now?"

"Sometimes, in my spare time. It's just a hobby." She glanced outside, and the scenery began to register. "Are we going back to your house?"

"I said I'd take you to breakfast on the way to the airport," he said as he parked and quickly stepped out of the car, before she could speak.

When she stepped out, she shook a finger at him. "On the way to the airport, my eye! Look at a map, buster."

"I'd rather look at a lovely lady," he said in a husky voice, pulling her into his arms.

She slipped easily out of his grasp and walked to the kitchen door. "You promised breakfast, not complications."

He held out his hands, palms up in innocence. "What do you mean by complications?"

"As you would say, let's discuss it over breakfast."

He laughed and unlocked the door, opening it for her. "The view is gorgeous outside, but just so you'll see that I don't mind people in my house, we're eating in the kitchen."

"You proved your point last night. Let's eat outside. I'll help you move things. I love to eat outside at home and watch the river."

"That muddy old river has been flowing quietly past Natchez forever. Don't you get tired of looking at it?"

"No, because I wonder about the people going up and down it on boats, and I think about the people who traveled it back in the past when Natchez was such an important town. The Mississippi could never be just a muddy old river to me," she said, picking up plates and glasses. "You shouldn't have gone to all this trouble," she said softly, admiring the bright blue place mats and pale blue napkins, white china, and a vase of roses in the center.

"This is a special morning." He winked, then turned to get a pitcher of orange juice and a pot of coffee. He brought out a crystal bowl of fruit, chunks of cantaloupe, strawberries, blackberries, banana, and fresh pineapple. Then he toasted English muffins and poured cups of steaming coffee while Hilary set the table on the terrace. She watched his strong hands move over the dishes; she noticed the creases in his cheeks when he laughed, and the flash of his white teeth.

After breakfast he leaned back in his chair and said, "Look, you must have had someone run the shop for you while you were here. Stay just another couple of days and let me show you around."

She was tempted—sorely tempted. Each time he asked, it was a bigger temptation, but she knew she could walk away now with her heart intact. If she stayed much longer, she wasn't so sure.

"It's too dangerous here," she said lightly. "Dynamite in hidden places . . . getting swept off my feet when I least expect it."

"There were warning signs," he answered. "You weren't afraid yesterday."

"Yesterday I wasn't aware of the dangers I faced. Now I am."

"There isn't a stick of dynamite anywhere around here," Brink drawled in a husky voice, giving his words a wildly sensual message.

The wind caught stray tendrils of her hair, blowing them against her cheek, and the sunlight revealed the flawless perfection of her skin. He had never been so drawn to a woman before in his life.

She was proving to be a marvelous companion. He enjoyed talking with her, teasing her. The thought that she would walk out of his life forever in just a few more hours was unthinkable. His gaze slipped down, lowering to look at the soft contours of her blue chambray shirt. The atmosphere between them tingled with tension as he saw the faint outline of her nipples; he knew that she was as stirred as he.

When his gaze flicked up to meet hers, he noted the slight flush on her cheeks, the smoldering yet hesitant look in her eyes. He was on fire, throbbing with need. With a scrape he pushed back his chair, reached for her wrist, and pulled gently.

"Let me show you my house," he invited.

Yet when they stood face-to-face, he was unable to do anything except struggle with the compelling urge to crush her in his arms.

"The grand tour," she prompted in a voice so breathless, he barely understood her. "And then I have to go."

"You don't really have to go. Just give us a week-end together, Hilary."

"*You* should have to wear a warning sign," she whispered.

"There's nothing dangerous about me," he replied, though he knew the kind of sweet danger she was referring to. He was unable to resist her. The word *seduction* was beginning to take on a whole new meaning to him. With Hilary it would be a glorious celebration of passion. He wanted to make love to her until she was clinging to him and crying out to him. Her lashes fluttered, and he wondered how much of his desire showed in his expression. When he noticed another flutter and a sweeping glance below his belt, her cheeks became pinker, and he became more determined than ever to get her into his bed. This woman made his pulse race in a manner that no woman had been able to do before in his life. The little antique dealer from Mississippi. A Wakefield. And she thought *he* should wear a warning sign!

"There are better things to do than stand here and stare at each other," he said dryly, taking her arm and leading her toward the sliding glass doors to his bedroom.

"Brink, I have to go, or I'll miss my plane. Please let my aunts buy the house."

"You are beautiful, dazzling, tantalizing, sexy, but no."

She couldn't be angry, not when his slightest touch melted her heart. His gaze dropped to her mouth, and she knew this time he was most definitely going to kiss her. Torn with mixed emotions, she watched him, half afraid of entanglements with him, half afraid of a bleak life without such entanglements.

He rubbed his hands up and down her arms. "Hilary Wakefield, unforgettable, sexy . . ."

With each word his voice lowered until it was a raspy whisper that played over her nerves like warm fingers.

Brink stared at her, aching with longing. He leaned down, noting the flicker of her lashes and the slight, eager lift of her face as she turned her lips up to his. His tongue played across hers, and she kissed him passionately in return.

He throbbed with desire, crushing her against him, wanting to kiss her until the damn plane was gone and the argument settled. A moment later he swept her up in his arms and carried her inside. "This is my bedroom," he whispered.

Hilary felt like she was on a roller coaster that had just topped the first hill and was starting its dizzying, uncontrollable descent.

"Brink, you go too fast. Or not fast enough. We have to leave for the airport."

He set her on her feet at the foot of his king-size bed. Her eyes were wide, filled with longing and desire. "We have something very special when we're together," he said.

"I know. But if it's real, we'll see each other again," she said, not believing her words for a minute. Half a continent separated them. She turned away quickly. "I have to go now, Brink, or I'll miss my plane."

"Airport it is," he said solemnly, feeling an uncustomary loss. He couldn't recall wanting someone so badly, or feeling so hurt by her saying good-bye to him so calmly. He shouldn't care. He had only known her twenty-four hours now. She was a Wakefield. She was as stubborn as a mule. But she had the damnedest effect on him!

Hilary picked up her purse. "We won't have time to do the dishes."

"I wouldn't have let you, anyway." He took her arm, wondering at the gruffness in his voice. She had turned his life topsy-turvy, and he wasn't reacting to anything in his customary way. They walked to his black Lincoln in silence, and he drove swiftly.

"When will we see each other again?" he asked.

"How can I answer a question like that!" she replied with amusement that grated on his raw nerves. She was a storm in his life, and he couldn't understand it! Usually he was the one in control; usually he was calm with women, happy with them, not at a loss, as he was now.

As soon as she checked in at the boarding gate, they called the flight, and he wanted to swear out loud. Then she was facing him. "I guess this is good-bye. I wish you'd think about Saville some more. It's just a house, Brink. I'm talking about people. Hearts and souls." She ran her finger along his tie, the touch tickling his chest in a delicious way. Then she looked up at him with a direct, wide-eyed stare that seemed to draw him closer.

"I'm scared of what's happening between us," she whispered.

Brink felt as if his heart suddenly had stopped beating. For a moment the commotion of milling people and the noise of boarding announcements were forgotten. He was lost in her wide green eyes, knowing she felt the same wild excitement he experienced.

"I want to make love to you," he said in a husky voice, leaning closer. "And someday, Hilary, I will. That's a promise. Fly off to your safe, familiar home, but I'm not saying good-bye."

His words rocked Hilary with all the force of a violent tremor. His gaze swept over her, as if peeling away every stitch of clothing, then returned to her mouth. With a sudden sweep, he lifted her to him, kissing her with a passion that merely reinforced his words.

Her heart thudded with strange new emotions. She didn't dare believe they would see each other again, but she did believe his statement, and his kisses set her aflame. Forgetting the bustling airport around them, she clung to him and returned his kiss.

When the final boarding call was announced, Brink released her and walked her to the boarding ramp.

"See you soon."

"Sure, Brink."

"Stay away from dynamite."

"I intend to," she answered solemnly. "I don't want to get hurt."

He frowned and caught her hand, pulling her back to him, causing her to bump into a boarding passenger.

"I'm sorry!" she exclaimed. The man smiled, nodding and giving Brink a curious glance.

"What's the crack about getting hurt? I'm no heartbreaker!"

"Whoo!" She winked at him, not believing for a second his solemn, pained expression. "I'll bet you have a date tonight, and by this time a month from now, you'll barely remember me."

"What do you want to bet?"

"Ma'am, they just gave the last call for boarding," the stewardess said, staring openly at Brink.

"Bet me something—a week out here as my guest if you lose."

"You're crazy!" she exclaimed.

"I don't drive over dynamite! If I forget you, you win, and I'll send you three gorgeous antiques for your shop!"

She laughed. "If you forget me, you'll never remember to buy three antiques!"

"Send me a note and remind me at Christmas!"

"You're nuts! And they're waiting on me!"

"Scared to bet?"

"It's a deal!" she called as she turned to run toward the door of the plane. She was still smiling broadly when she rushed down the aisle to her seat. She stared out the window at the airport, knowing Brink was inside. It had only been a few days since she had left Natchez, yet it seemed years ago. Had there been a life before Brink?

There had, she thought, mentally answering her question. And there would be again, and she was going to get three gorgeous antiques for the shop the first of next year. She laughed softly, thinking over the last few wild minutes with him. He was different from any man she had ever known. Forceful, dynamic, intelligent, rash, high-tempered, sexy. Oh, how sexy!

And she knew she was in his thoughts too. It wouldn't last long, but for the time being, it warmed her to picture him driving home and mulling over their moments together. And they had shared some very special moments.

She watched the traffic below, looking at the sprawling city, trying to spot Brink's house, hating the distance that was swiftly spreading between them. Yet it had been best to leave. He was a heartbreaker deluxe! A brief moment in his arms had reminded Hilary of all the dazzling excitement her life had lacked. Frowning, she forced the thought out of her mind. She had a wonderful, peaceful life with no need for a man like Brink Claiborn, a man who would constantly stir up a whirlwind of danger.

By the time she changed planes in Houston, catching the Royale commuter flight to the nearest town, Alexandria, Louisiana, and driving home the last sixty-five miles to Natchez, she was more in control, having sobered over the prospect of telling her aunts about the failure of her mission. Ambivalent feelings warred inside her when she thought of Saville and Brink. How could he think only of an empty old house when two little ladies' hearts and happiness were at stake! Men! One particular man, at least.

When she turned the last mile, winding up the road to her house, worry and dread set in. How would she explain her failure to her dear aunts?

To her dismay, the ladies were waiting expectantly in her driveway, sitting in their vintage 1963 pink Cadillac. Both had been widowed long ago and lived together now in Mavis's home where she had always lived with her husband, Tom Johnson. Tall and thin with gray hair pulled back severely into a bun, Sophie Wakefield Brown stepped out first, smoothing her severe navy crepe dress. Mavis walked beside her. Almost a foot shorter than Sophie, Mavis's wild orange-red curls and flashy red-and-yellow flowered dress were a contrast to Sophie's stark appearance. Both women waited with eager curiosity, and there was such a glimmer of hope in their eyes that Hilary's feelings about Brink began to waver.

"He's a damn Merlin," she mumbled to herself, and reached out to hug Sophie, then Mavis.

"Darling, we can't ever thank you enough!" Mavis gushed. "Tell us what he said!"

Five

Hilary's heart sank as she looked into their hopeful faces. Damn Brink Claiborn, she thought.

"I finally got to see him. He's thinking about it, but so far he hasn't agreed," she said, trying to break the bad news as gently as possible.

The changes in their emotions were as evident as the river sweeping around the bend. Mavis's eyes filled with tears; Sophie frowned. Their smiles faded, their shoulders slumped, and Hilary wanted to shake Brink Claiborn!

"I'm sorry," she said, "but Brink is—"

"Brink?" Sophie asked, her frown deepening.

"Mr. Claiborn is stubborn, unreasonable, and impossible." Not to mention sexy and adorable, she thought. As a consolation, she added, "Don't worry, I'll try again."

Both aunts sniffed and got out their handkerchiefs.

"Come inside and sit down. We'll eat some ice cream, and I'll tell you about my trip."

After the ladies had settled on the sofa with bowls of chocolate and strawberry ice cream, Hilary excused herself.

"I'll be right back. I need to make a business call."

She closed the door to her bedroom, walked to the phone, and placed a person-to-person call to Brink Claiborn at the office of Claiborn Industries. She had the number memorized.

She caught him in the office. His secretary answered, and it took only seconds to get through to him. His deep voice was soothing, almost like a rain shower falling on her steaming temper. Almost.

"How can you be so damn coldhearted!"

"Hilary! Are you here?"

"No, I'm not in L.A.! I just arrived home, and my aunts were here to greet me. They're sitting in my living room, crying as if their hearts were broken, and it's all your fault. I pity your poor grandfather or anyone else who is going to be cared for by you, Mr. Cold-as-Marble Claiborn." Before he could respond, she hung up.

She felt better until she went back to sit with her aunts. The ladies wore such gloomy expressions, Hilary's temper began to rise again. While her emotions churned, she wondered what it was about Brink that made her lose all control. She had always considered herself a placid person. Everyone described her as sweet; even Brink had done that. *What a sweet child . . . you're a sweet girl. . . .* She had heard that all her life. A little impulsive, she had to admit, but hot-tempered? Never! Until Brink entered her life. She realized that Sophie and Mavis were staring at her.

"Hilary, are you well?"

"Yes, of course!"

"You haven't heard a word we said. Lucinda is coming for tea tomorrow, and she wanted to know if you had found the silver tea service she's been looking to acquire."

"I'm sorry. I was worrying about Saville and Brink Claiborn," Hilary said half truthfully.

Finally she kissed her aunts good night and promised to talk to Brink again, although she thought it an impossible task.

The house seemed empty, and she was restless. She called her friend, Scott Blair, to tell him she was back in town and was relieved to make a date for Saturday night. Perhaps then she could get every last bit of Brink out of her memory.

It didn't work out that way. Blond and handsome, Scott should have driven away the unwanted longing for the dangerous man in Los Angeles, but then she and Scott had never had that electric attraction between them. They had been friends since high school, never lovers, never soul mates. And while she sat at dinner with Scott, she couldn't help but wonder who Brink was out with. Kiki, perhaps?

Sunday morning she drove her aunts to church, then treated them to a lovely brunch at an inn high on the hill overlooking the river.

Afterward, as they turned up the narrow, cracked driveway toward Aunt Mavis's house, Hilary noted the profusion of pink, purple, red, and white azaleas in riotous bloom. While she went along the walk from the car to the back door, she breathed deeply. Brink was wrong. The tall old oaks were draped with graceful Spanish moss. The flowers were gorgeous, and the house old and charming, with its wide gallery beneath a steeply sloping roof, the fan transoms over doors and windows, the white picket fence almost hidden by flowers.

Inside the house, the kitchen had twelve-foot-high ceilings, with glass-fronted cabinets and a fan turning slowly overhead. The stove and refrigerator were old, but the room held a quaint charm. Maybe it could use a coat of paint, but that wasn't anything to get excited about.

"I think it's time we all had a little nap," Mavis said.

"You go right ahead. I didn't get to finish reading the paper this morning. Have you seen the paper, Hilary? I saw an ad for a dress that looks perfect for you. Come in and let me show you."

Hilary looked at the ad but couldn't really imagine herself in the dress with big poppies all over it. Still restless, she excused herself and wandered down the hall with its cypress floor, Oriental throw rugs, and mahogany woodwork. To her amazement, she saw that there were cobwebs in the corners, wrinkles in the faded old wallpaper, and chipped, peeling varnish on the moldings. The spacious south bedroom, its windows open to views of blooming azaleas, was one of her favorite rooms. She had spent many nights there as a child. Now she noticed the tattered lace curtains, the cracked walls, the spots and dust and cobwebs, suddenly seeing it clearly, vividly.

It was painful, like taking a close look at someone she loved and realizing that they had grown old. But she owed Brink an apology of sorts, because he was right about the house. It was run-down. She hadn't realized how badly. In the past few years she'd seldom stayed for more than a few hours at a time, and she'd simply taken her surroundings for granted, always enjoying Mavis and Sophie, their beautiful antiques, and their gorgeous yard. Often they just sat in the rocking chairs on the porch, talking with neighbors who would stroll by, listening to the birds, and enjoying life.

As she went through room after room, Hilary found the same conditions. So many things were worn, faded, chipped, or cracked. Later she drove home to her house, which seemed *empty*. It never had seemed empty before meeting Brink—before B.C., as she was beginning to relate every aspect of her life to him, B.C. and A.D. Before Claiborn and After Devastation, because that seemed to be the new focus of her life: surviving the aftermath and adjusting to the devastating results of her encounter with him!

That evening, while she sat on her patio and watched the river, Hilary came to some conclusions. Brink had been right about the condition of her aunts' house. It was in disrepair, but everything could be remedied easily. She would hire a maid to clean once a week, and a handyman to put up fresh wallpaper and a coat of new paint. She knew her aunts had more than enough money to fix up their house without causing them the slightest hardship, but they were frugal. She would just have to convince them that they needed to do a few repairs as time went by.

Brink intended to redo Saville, anyway, so she was still firm in her feeling that he was being cold and callous about her aunts. They might not keep their home as meticulous as he thought they should, but they were warm, loving ladies. She was right back to wondering how he could consider an empty old house more important than two lovable ladies. Of course, they might not seem so lovable to Brink, but they were human beings! Not just boards and bricks.

But Hilary hadn't heard a word from Brink since she had hung up on him. She had probably sent his temper soaring. Too bad! she thought. She shook her head, watching the paddle wheeler chug around the bend with its load of tourists. It was the majestic *Delta Queen* riverboat, headed upriver to St. Louis.

And something else bothered her. She wondered if Brink's grandfather, Carlton Claiborn, was lonesome. Brink was his only living relative, and he was seldom home. On impulse she called Sunny Meadows and asked if Carlton was able to have visitors. She was told that he could. Hilary decided to stop by the nursing home on her way home from work the following day.

The tall, gaunt man who sat propped in bed was frail, elderly, and very ill, but his eyes were sharp and he seemed interested in the young woman seated at his side. She told him about visiting Brink, relating only that it had been nice to meet his grandson and that they had had a long talk about Saville. She had to talk loudly, because Carlton Claiborn's hearing aid didn't seem to do a lot of good.

His speech was halting, but he talked a little about the house, about old times. She didn't want to tire him, so she told him good-bye after half an hour.

During the week, whenever she saw a tall, broad-shouldered, brown-haired man walk into the shop, Hilary's heart jumped in the most jarring manner. And her sleep was ruined! Only twenty-four hours with Brink and the effect was devastating! Determined to get that man off her mind, Hilary prepared a new canvas to paint in her spare hours. Perhaps she could lose herself in a seascape and forget about Brink.

On Friday she realized it had been one week since she had told him good-bye at the airport. Even Becky and Nan, two of her employees, had noticed something amiss. Small wonder that they had, she thought dryly as she moved around the shop on Friday afternoon.

The antique store was well situated, on the southeast corner of a downtown block in an old two-story building. The shop was light and airy, with wide glass windows allowing natural sunlight in to dance and glimmer upon the multitude of crystal in the shop.

Hilary hummed as she dusted, enjoying a momentary lull. When she'd slipped on her white piqué dress that morning, she had been amazed to discover she had lost weight. She knew her appetite had diminished, but she hadn't realized to what extent. The bell over the doorway tinkled, and Scott entered, dimples showing in his cheeks as he smiled at her.

"Busy?" he asked, combing his thick blond hair away from his tanned face with his fingers.

"Right now it's quiet. The last busload of tourists is gone for today."

"Good. I've got the tickets for the concert tonight."

"Great! I'm ready to relax."

"Yeah, I quit early this afternoon and thought I'd stop by and tell you."

Hilary looked outside as a black car slowed and pulled into an open space in front of the shop. A man stepped out to drop a coin in the meter, then came striding through the door, making the little brass bell jingle again. She dropped her feather duster and tried to ignore the wild beat of her heart as she noticed Brink Claiborn standing before her, sporting an irresistible grin.

Six

Dressed in a navy summer suit and navy tie, Brink looked breathtakingly handsome. Although he glanced back and forth between Scott and Hilary, the smile on his face was for her. She couldn't believe Brink was really in her shop, coming toward her.

Silently Brink swore. One look at the handsome blond guy talking to Hilary and he realized he should have called her first, but he hadn't known whether or not he could get away from Los Angeles until the last possible minute. As it was, they had held the plane for him for a few minutes.

Hilary looked great! Brink's pulse raced, and he wished he could pull her into his arms and kiss her here and now. The mere sight of her answered the question that had plagued him during the long trip to Natchez: Was Hilary Wakefield really as dazzling as he had remembered her to be?

She was. Her white dress was crisp and fresh, the vee neckline revealing enticing curves.

"Hi!" she said breathlessly, blinking and staring for a moment.

"Hi. I should have called, but I had to rush." Tension arced between them, wreaking havoc with his senses. He wanted to give the blond stranger a shove and tell him to beat it. What was it about this woman that brought out the most primitive reactions in him?

"Brink, this is Scott Blair. Scott, Brink Claiborn."

"Glad to meet you. Your grandfather owns Saville. I've heard about you from Hilary," he said cheerfully, giving Brink a firm handshake.

Handsome *and* friendly. Brink wanted to gnash his teeth. "I thought I'd better come see my grandfather. He hasn't been too well lately."

"We heard. Sorry about that, but Hilary went to see him yesterday and said she had a nice visit."

Brink stared at her in surprise. She had gone to see his grandfather, the crotchety grouch who never had liked visitors?

"I thought I should come talk to Hilary and her aunts about Saville too," Brink said, suddenly amazed at his own words. That was the last thing he had intended to do in Natchez! What was the matter with him? He could handle business deals with poise and finesse and cool logic—qualities he seemed to have left behind in Los Angeles.

"Are you going to be in Natchez long?" Scott asked with the friendly persistence of a puppy.

"No, I'm not. This is just a quick trip," Brink answered, unable to take his gaze from Hilary's.

"Well, I'm taking Hilary to a concert tonight. I bought a block of tickets for my office, so if you'd like to join us, we'd be glad to have you."

Brink saw the look of shock cross Hilary's features,, and it matched his own reaction. The last thing he wanted to do was play the fifth wheel on a date with Hilary. "Thanks a lot, but I have some other plans."

"Too bad. It's Kenny Rogers and Merle Haggard, and the concert is sold out. These are front row seats too."

"How nice."

"Brink, if you'll just wait in the office, right back there," Hilary said, to his relief, "Scott and I'll be through with our plans in just a minute."

"He doesn't need to go," Scott said in the same cheerful tone. Brink took a deep breath and tried to hang on to his patience while Scott continued, "I'll pick you up at six for dinner. How's that? Want to join us for dinner?"

"Thanks, anyway," Brink answered with a negative shake of his head.

"Sorry you can't go. It's going to be a great evening." He turned back to Hilary. "Want to eat at your favorite, The Briars? Or the West Bank Eatery in Vidalia?"

"The West Bank sounds great."

"Ginger and Zack are going."

"Good."

"It was real nice to meet you," Scott said to Brink. "See you, hon."

Hon. Brink realized that his hand was jammed into his trouser pocket and clenched into a fist.

"Bye, Scott."

They both watched Scott weave carefully past the antiques on his way to the door. As he opened it, Sophie entered.

"Hi, Miss Sophie," Scott greeted her. "Guess who's in town to see you?"

Brink wondered what he had done wrong to bring on such a lousy turn of events in his life.

"Who's that?" she asked.

"Brink Claiborn."

Her face lit up, and Brink swore mentally. Both the aunts and Hilary were going to think he had changed his mind if he didn't let them know differently at once. He had not flown from Los Angeles to make a deal with the Wakefield sisters!

He turned around, whispering, "I have *not* changed my mind about Saville!"

"Why're you here?" Hilary asked as Scott closed the door.

"How wonderful for you to fly to Natchez to see us," Sophie exclaimed, grabbing his arm before he had a chance to answer Hilary.

"Yes, ma'am," he replied politely. Both of the women were waiting expectantly. "I thought tomorrow morning we might sit down and talk," he said, again shocked at himself. Being around Hilary was like dealing with live electrical wires. His mental processes became jolted and scrambled.

"How nice!" Both women beamed at him, and he jammed his other hand into his pocket.

"I just was passing by and thought I would stop in," Sophie said happily. "I'm so glad I did. Now we'll just plan a little luncheon for everyone tomorrow. I must run home and tell Mavis. She'll be so thrilled. Mr. Claiborn, I can't tell you how happy I am that you're here. And I'm sure Hilary is, too, aren't you, dear?"

"Of course," she murmured, laughter dancing in her eyes.

"See you tomorrow. How about eleven o'clock, Mr. Claiborn?"

"Fine," Brink ground out with forced politeness.

As soon as Sophie went out the door, Hilary burst out with a merry laugh. "You look just as furious as you did the day you carried me off your work site!"

"I didn't come to Natchez to see your aunts or spend an evening with you and your damn good-looking date!" His temper was rising again, and he tried to subdue it before it was too late.

"Scott's a good friend, and I think he's a very friendly person."

"Yeah, so I noticed."

"He isn't hot-tempered or grouchy or stubborn. He adapts."

"That's just wonderful. I'm afraid I'll disappoint your aunts tomorrow, because I didn't come to see them or talk about Saville."

"Then maybe you and I don't have any reason to see each other, either."

Now he was on familiar ground. He moved closer, reaching around her to brace his hand against a counter, hemming her in.

"We have the best reason in the world," he said, lowering his voice to an intimate tone. He saw the change in her features as he leaned closer, heard the quick intake of her breath as he studied her lovely features.

"I can't break my date with Scott. It's a special evening for him; he's a big Kenny Rogers fan."

"I don't expect you to break your date," he said, touching her collar. She smelled as sweet and enticing as he remembered. He wanted to kiss her, but instead, he continued, "I should have let you know I was coming. I should have called from Alexandria."

"That's all right. But why are you here, if it's not about Saville?"

"Do you really have to ask?" he whispered, leaning close to brush her lips with his. His heart seemed to stop. It was as wonderful to kiss her as he had remembered! It was better than he had remembered! "You're addictive," he murmured.

"I'm also at work!" she said, slipping under his arm and stepping away from him. "You'll start a scandal."

"Natchez can weather a scandal, or it would have disappeared from the face of the earth long ago. And what's this I hear about you going to see Grandpa?"

"I felt sorry for the old gentleman. You're his only relative, and how often do you visit?"

"Well, it's a little difficult to get here from Los Angeles."

"Is it?"

"Why are you getting angry?"

"I'm not. Well, maybe a little. If you can come winging out here to see me, you can do it for your grandfather too."

"How in sweet hell do you know how seldom or how often I come to Natchez?"

"Oh, I always hear from my aunts."

"I forget what towns this size are like."

"This town is absolutely grand!" She waved her hand at the wide, tree-lined street that had very little traffic. "You want to swap that for a Los Angeles freeway?"

It was his turn to laugh. "Why do I feel a thunderstorm brewing every time we try to talk?"

She laughed, and his heartbeat quickened. He was glad he had come. "When can we get together?" he asked. "Tomorrow afternoon? Tomorrow night?"

She smoothed his tie, running her fingers along the lapel of his coat. Her touch transported him. Suddenly the walls seemed to close in around him; the temperature soared to a steamy jungle heat.

"I'd like that. I have the day off tomorrow, anyway."

Her lips looked so delectable, her eyes so enchanting. He had to be alone with her. "Show me your office."

Her eyes widened in surprise, and then her lashes fluttered. Did she understand his intentions? he wondered. Without a word she turned and led him back past a group of antiques. Normally he would have wanted to study the fine collectibles, but now he was oblivious to them.

They went through a back door, down a hallway, and into a room comfortably decorated with a desk, a cheerful-looking yellow chintz love seat, two green metal file cabinets, two tan vinyl chairs, and a work table. He closed the door behind him, his pulse racing as she waited, ripe for his kiss. She was so sexy, so sensual, the mere sight of her made his blood heat. He swept her into his arms.

Just as eagerly, her arms slid around his neck and they kissed wildly, both yielding to the longing they felt. She set him on fire. His aching need for her surged through him like a raging inferno. She trembled but managed to wind her fingers through his hair, pulling him closer.

He burned with a desperate urgency, a compulsion. "I've thought about you constantly," he finally whispered.

"And I couldn't forget you, Brink," she replied breathlessly.

"What is it that happens when we're together?" he asked, showering kisses on her neck, letting his hand drift down her back and over her enticing curves. His fingers lingered, slowly massaging her lower back, moving in a lazy circle.

She moaned softly, her hips moving against him.

Brink had to fight to maintain control.

"It's never happened to me before," she answered honestly, leaning back to look up at him with those soulful green eyes.

He had to have her all to himself, in a quiet, private place. "What would happen if you locked up early?"

"Nothing." She smiled at him. "That's a marvelous idea."

She constantly amazed him. He would have expected her to argue or protest, to be a stickler for convention and schedules, but she had agreed immediately. He watched as she straightened a few papers, then picked up her purse. "My car's in back."

"Mine's in front. Leave yours here."

She nodded, and he followed her through the store. Before they stepped outside, she turned the sign on the front door to read CLOSED in bold, black letters. Then she locked up and climbed into his car.

Whistling, he pulled off his coat and went around to climb in behind the wheel. "I can't believe you went to see Grandpa."

"I did, and he seemed to enjoy it."

"Of course he would! What man wouldn't, even if he is in his nineties?"

When she laughed, he reached across to squeeze her hand.

"Want to see my home?" she asked.

"Give me directions."

"Turn right at the corner."

He drove through town, then turned when she directed, the car climbing the winding road on the bluff overlooking the river.

"My view will be a letdown after the panoramic view from your house," she said when they entered a back hallway.

"*Au contraire,*" he answered lightly, catching her arm and turning her to face him. "The view here is exactly what I traveled over nineteen hundred miles to see," he said, his voice suddenly raspy with emotion. "And I can't wait one minute longer," he added, tilting her face up to his, lowering his head to kiss her, plundering her delicious lips.

"I had to see you again," he whispered finally, framing her delicate face with his hands. She caught his wrists lightly.

"You're going too fast. Nothing like this has happened to me before."

"Me, either," he said, concerned by her solemn expression. This was a special lady. He knew that she would not tolerate a casual commitment. She was the kind who had marriage written all over her. He shook his head, wanting to prolong this glorious moment, but compelled to admit that he wasn't the marrying kind.

She tilted her head to study him. "What's wrong?"

"You look like the wedding-band, vine-covered-cottage type," he admitted, unable to resist saying it aloud.

"And that scares you?"

"A little," he answered honestly, "although I'm not the womanizer you seem to think."

"Somehow I got a different impression." She laughed and hugged him lightly, resting her head against his chest.

He looked down at her crown of shining golden hair. He wanted to hold her forever, to make love to her, to kiss every inch of her. He raised her face. "I'm not kidding. There really haven't been all that many women in my past. And there hasn't been any one special for some time."

She eyed him skeptically, then took his hand. "Come see my view."

Brink felt as if he had just had a narrow escape. Since his first encounter with her, he'd fluctuated between wanting her desperately and reminding himself that she was a Wakefield and not his type.

Hilary's house was cozy and contemporary, with glass and teak furniture, a pile of colorful, overstuffed cushions, and two blue directors' chairs. Brink was impressed by her small collection of oil paintings. He was unequivocally moved by one canvas hanging above the hearth, an intriguing portrait of a child on a beach.

"But there isn't an antique in this place—except for that grandfather clock," he remarked.

"I spend every day surrounded by antiques. At home, it's nice to have a change."

She pushed open sliding doors that led to a deck built over the edge of the bluff. Below was the wide Mississippi River, its swirling waves glistening in the sunshine. Across the ribbon of water lay the flatlands of Louisiana.

"An absolutely incredible view!" he said softly, mesmerized. When he finally looked away, he noticed an
easel with the acrylic painting of a beach. It was
precisely detailed, yet sweeping and dreamy—amazingly
good. He had guessed that Hilary dabbled in painting, but this work was of professional quality, with
balance and depth and an unusual blend of color.

"You're really good!"

"Thank you," she said, smiling with pleasure. She
pulled up two canvas chairs.

"I knew that scene looked familiar. You've done
an interpretation of my beach," he said with
satisfaction.

A startled look crossed her features as her cheeks
became pink. She blinked, staring at her painting.
"It is your beach. That's odd. I never even realized
what I was doing."

"How long are you going to fight what you feel
with me?"

"I don't think I've fought much at all, unless you're
referring to hopping into bed. You were right, Brink.
That isn't my style."

"That wasn't what I meant. I know that isn't your
style. But you're fighting this attraction between us,
before it even has a chance to grow. Think about
how you hightailed it out of L.A."

She shrugged and turned away. He wanted to hold
her, to reassure her, but he couldn't.

As they sat on her patio talking, Brink felt as if he
could pour out all his private desires and ambitions
and worries to her. And he wanted to hear hers, to
learn all about her. Far too soon, he knew he had to
leave.

"I'll go now so you can get ready for your date, dammit!"

She stood up with him and laughed, linking her arm through his. "While we're both calm and cool, I'll show you the rest of my house."

Once inside, he pointed to the painting he'd noticed before. "Who's the little girl in this piece?"

"Hilary Mae Larson, my best friend's child. She's named after me. The beach was improvised. I sketched that when she was standing in her sandbox."

"It's quite good. Why are you selling antiques when you paint so well?"

"Art is such an insecure profession, highly competitive. You compete with others; you compete with yourself. Selling antiques is peaceful and relaxing."

He stared at her in dismay. "That's crazy! If I had your talent, hell and high water couldn't keep me from pursuing a career in art."

"No, I don't imagine it would stop you," she said evenly. "You're very forceful, probably competitive and aggressive. Many men are, but I'm not. I don't want to fight my way through life."

"If you were average or mediocre, I could understand your answer, but, damn, you're really good."

She laughed. "I'm no Matisse or Rembrandt! There are millions of artists better than I am!"

"You're wrong," he said quietly. "I've studied and collected art. There's no way for you to convince me you're not enormously talented. You shouldn't let your fear of competition hold you back."

"I'm not afraid of it; I just don't want any part of it. I don't want the hassle. Now, do you want to see the rest of the house? Scott will be here soon, and I have to dress."

"Dammit! I want to take you out tonight. I know it's not your fault and I should have called, but I couldn't. And, yes, show me the rest of your place."

"Right this way, sir," she said lightly.

He had to laugh as he followed her, watching the slight, provocative sway of her hips, the rounded contours of her bottom.

Her bedroom was decorated with bamboo furniture, an overhead fan, a water bed, and thick, beige wall-to-wall carpeting. He also noticed rows of finished canvases stacked against one wall.

"It's beautiful. Now I'll be able to picture you asleep. I've never slept on a water bed."

"I don't believe it!" she said, folding her arms across her middle as he sauntered over, sat on her bed, and bounced on it lightly.

Hilary watched him cautiously, her pulse jumping as he stretched out across her bed. She knew she would remember that image always. Her room would never seem quite the same.

He rolled over and reached out to pull her down on his lap.

"Brink—"

"Shh, Hilary. I lied. I just wanted to see how you look in bed. When I call you long-distance, I'll know."

"That—"

He kissed her, silencing her words. She clung to him, lost in a giddy spiral that made her forget reason and logic.

After a moment she stood up. "Scott's coming, remember?"

He laughed and caressed her chin lightly with his forefinger. "Don't worry, I'm going! I know I've overstayed my welcome. How about eleven o'clock in the morning?"

"Fine," she said as she walked to the door with him. "Where are you staying?"

"At Saville."

"You are?"

"Don't sound so horrified. You really don't like old houses, do you?"

"I like them. I just don't want to live in one, ever again."

"I'm just spending a night, not moving in permanently," he said, frowning.

"We're so different," she said softly, knowing he was thinking the same thing.

He nodded. "Maybe opposites attract, because that's one thing we have to agree on—attraction." He took her in his arms again and held her. "I haven't been able to sleep since I met you. And I've had trouble making decisions at work, a first for me. I think about you, I miss you—"

"You can't!" She glanced at her watch. "Brink, I'm sorry, but I have only thirty minutes to get ready now."

"How I wish you were going out with me. I'll be thinking about you all night long." He paused in the doorway. "Would you mind if I called you late tonight?"

"No, you can call," she answered with amusement. "I should be home by two."

"Two?"

"You're beginning to sound like my father!" she said, then laughed.

He looked stricken. "Damned if I'm not! Sorry. I despise jealous women. Guess I'm being unfair to you."

He seemed so sincere, her amusement vanished. "It's okay, Brink. We do something . . . strange to each other," she whispered, awed and scared.

"Yeah," he said gruffly. "That we do." With that he was gone, striding swiftly to his car, looking rugged and handsome.

Hilary was stunned at the day's revelations. She and Brink brought out unique qualities in each other. Their attraction was monumental, but was it lasting? She knew that he didn't want a permanent commitment at this time in his life. And she couldn't live with a casual one. Although she liked modern furniture, she was as old-fashioned as her 110-year-old grandfather clock when it came to relationships.

The drone of an engine warned her that Scott was coming up the drive. She was late!

Seven

Hilary ran through the house, yanking down the zipper to the white piqué, then pulling on a white shirt and blue jeans. She was brushing her hair when the door bell rang. She twisted and looped the tendrils atop her head and threw open the door.

"I'm sorry, I'm running late," she said, holding her hair up and slipping in another pin.

"I passed your friend, Brink. If you wanted to go out with him tonight, Hilary, you could have. There's a whole group going to the concert, and I told Meredith she could ride with us."

"That's fine. And this is fine. I want to go to the concert," she said politely. "Give me just two minutes."

He caught her arm and turned her to face him. "Hon, we've known each other a long time. If you want to go out with Brink Claiborn, I have someone who'd like this ticket."

She studied Scott's wide blue eyes. She knew he

was sincere, but every minute she spent near Brink was volatile, often beyond control. Did she really want such an explosive evening?

"Are you sure?"

"Positive," he said with a grin and a twinkle in his eyes.

"Who's going to use my ticket?" she asked, suddenly realizing that he was unduly pleased.

"Somebody I met yesterday at the grocery."

"At the grocery!"

He grinned. "Yeah, she's new in town."

"Use my phone if you want to call her," Hilary said dryly.

"Thanks." He hurried to the phone, and Hilary went outside to sit down on the step to give him some privacy. As she pulled the pins from her hair, she wondered if she had just given up Kenny Rogers and Merle Haggard to spend the evening alone at home.

When Scott came out, his grin made it unnecessary for her to ask if his new friend had agreed to go with him.

"You're a sweetie," he said. "Thanks, Hilary."

"You're welcome. Introduce me to her sometime."

"I will. Maybe we can go on a picnic together next week."

"Sure, Scott," she said, amused at the rapid turn of events. For years Scott had wanted marriage and a family, but he hadn't found the right person. Hilary hoped this time he had, and she hoped the woman was as good as he deserved.

Perhaps the evening was meant to happen this way, she thought, picking up the phone to call Brink.

He would have had time to get to Saville if he had gone straight there.

When he didn't answer, she laughed at herself. "An evening alone for you, chump!" she said, then thought of his grandfather. He might have gone to the nursing home. She called Sunny Meadows and asked the nurse on duty if Mr. Claiborn's grandson was there. She was amused that no description was necessary.

"Yes, he is."

"Would you give him a message when he leaves?"

"Just a minute. I see him in the hall now."

A moment later Hilary heard Brink's deep voice. "Hello?"

"Hi."

"You're calling me from the concert?" he asked with surprise, recognizing her voice.

"No, I'm at home. I told you Scott's a good friend and very understanding."

"You asked him—"

"No, he asked me if I wanted to stay home instead. He saw you drive away."

"Scott is a fine, fine man. See, no jealousy at all! I'll pick you up in an hour. I'm tired of this suit. Care if it's casual tonight?"

"Not at all," she answered, a mental image coming to mind of him dressed in tight jeans, as he had been on their first meeting. No, she wouldn't mind at all. She probably wouldn't be able to keep her eyes off him!

"Bye, Brink."

Excitement surged through her. She would be with Brink—all evening. Once again she was skittering around on dynamite!

When he arrived on her doorstep, Hilary tried to hide the fact that her gaze was traveling over his strong, lean body. He looked marvelous in tight jeans and a blue cotton shirt.

As they drove down the hill he said, "It's been a long time since I've been in Natchez. Want to drive to town and just walk around a little?"

"Sure."

They walked through the town for an hour, strolling past historic homes that were on the Pilgrimage tour, pausing to look at the magnificent Georgian mansion, Rosalie, built by Peter Little on the bluffs where the French had first built Fort Rosalie in 1716.

Brink explained things about the house that she didn't know. It was built by James Griffin of Baltimore. General Grant had stayed there. Brink looked down at her, pushing a tendril of hair away from her cheek. "Are you sure you grew up here?"

"Yes. I got tired of listening to all the history."

"Hopeless, hopeless! This is one of the finest examples of Georgian architecture in Natchez." While Brink gazed at Rosalie's columns and double galleries, Hilary gazed at Brink. She thought he was one of the finest examples of the male gender she had ever seen!

He took her arm. "Right over there is the Parsonage."

"I know that much about my hometown!"

They walked across the street to let Brink look at the Parsonage, another house built by Peter Little for the ministers who were guests of his religious wife, Eliza.

As they strolled through the streets, they passed

playgrounds where Brink had played as a child, stores he knew.

"This is nice," he said.

"You sound envious."

"I'd forgotten how charming it is."

"Maybe you should wander more often."

"Yeah," he said, looking beyond her. "This is peaceful. Quiet."

"Quiet is boring for some people."

He wiggled his hand. "A little peace and quiet is nice. I haven't had much calm in my life for a long time now."

"Then this is good for you."

"It sure is," he said emphatically, gazing down at her.

"That's one of the things I like about living here," she continued. "My life is peaceful." *Or it was until a week ago!*

He laced his fingers in hers, and she felt a deep sense of contentment. They discussed books, and to her delight she discovered he'd read and enjoyed many of her favorite books.

"Want to come see Saville and eat at home?"

"Do you have groceries?"

"Nope. But we can buy some on the way."

"Sure."

"And you can show me where you grew up."

Surprised, she looked up at him. "It's just another old house. Not a fancy one like Rosalie. Just a house."

"It can't be just a house," he said, gazing at her with a hungry look that made her heart thud.

"You'll see." She gave him directions to the two-story frame house with a wide porch.

Brink pulled up in front of the house and cut off

the engine. "Which room was yours?" he asked, staring intently.

"The front corner."

"No brothers and sisters?"

"Nope. Just like you."

"One more thing we have in common," he said quietly, giving her a wink. "Let's go home."

His words sent a strange tingle through her. One wink and sparks skittered through her system. What was it between them that stirred such magic?

They stopped for groceries, and she was amazed at the amount of items he purchased, then they sped toward Saville. The wide wrought-iron gate was open at the entrance. The drive was lined with trees and vines amid a thick undergrowth of brambles and wild roses, which told of the recent lack of care. As they rounded the last bend the mansion came into view. The majestic redbrick structure had double galleries, six Doric columns, and fanlights over the door. And parked right in front, beside a magnolia tree, was a familiar pink Cadillac.

"I have company!" he said, amazed to see the car.

"My aunts."

"You're kidding! Aw, hell, that *is* their car! Sorry, Hilary, but I wanted you all to myself."

She had to smother a laugh. When he noticed, his scowl became more fierce. "Did you know they were coming?"

"Of course not! They may have been here waiting for you for hours."

"Dammit! I'm sorry, but you and your aunts are just as different as night and day. I want to see you as badly as I *don't* want to see them!"

She clamped her lips together to suppress a giggle.

"One saving grace—at least my attitude isn't making you angry. But stop laughing at me. Those ladies stick like glue."

"They also go to bed at ten-thirty"—she paused when he groaned, then continued—"right after the news. And they'll go home before dark, because they can't see to drive at night. Aunt Sophie and Aunt Mavis are such dears. You have a whole grouchy side to you, you know!"

He slowed behind the Cadillac. "Hilary, you're adorable. But your aunts are like flypaper. Here they come. Oh, Lordy, I don't deserve this!"

"Cheer up, Brink. You can handle anything."

She climbed out. "Hi, Aunt Sophie. Aunt Mavis."

"Hilary! What a pleasant surprise. We didn't dream you'd be here," Sophie said, casting a curious glance at Hilary and Brink. "We thought poor Mr. Claiborn would be alone and without food in the kitchen, so we brought dinner."

"Ladies, that's very thoughtful, but—"

"It's the least we could do," Mavis said, trying to lift a casserole dish from the backseat of the Cadillac. "We cooked for two hours. I do hope you like carrot-and-spinach soufflé."

Brink had to grit his teeth, and he saw Hilary duck her head. Why, oh why had fate wrought such a catastrophe in his life, causing him to fall in love with a Wakefield? *Fall in love?*

He gave Hilary a startled glance. She arched her brows in curiosity while he took the spinach-and-carrot soufflé from Mavis's hands.

"I'll carry the food, ladies. Why don't you go on inside."

Hilary picked up another covered dish, and they

all went up the broad steps and across the gallery. Brink unlocked the door and opened it wide. The aunts stepped inside first, then Hilary ducked beneath Brink's arm while he held the door for her.

"Spinach, carrots, and soufflés are abominations!" he whispered. "The only thing that's worse is turnip greens and hominy grits."

"My goodness, what happened to your Southern taste?" Hilary drawled as he followed her inside.

"We brought Hilary's favorite," Sophie said, waving her hand at the covered dish in her niece's hands.

"Let me guess," Brink snapped, taking one look at Hilary's twinkling eyes. Suddenly he had to laugh at himself. "Do I smell turnip greens or grits?"

"Turnip greens," all three ladies answered at once.

When they were alone in the kitchen, he turned to glower at her. "Will you stop laughing over this! How in hell can you like turnip greens? Your favorite?"

"Not really. I'll take jambalaya any day, but I like Aunt Sophie's greens and black-eyed peas and Aunt Mavis's fried okra."

"My nerves aren't ready for an evening with Miss Sophie and Miss Mavis." He shook his head. "It dumbfounds me. I've built a successful business from scratch. I manage a large staff, supervise contracts and jobs. But when it comes to the Wakefields, I'm a bumbling blob of jelly that gets squeezed and poked!"

"Squeezed and poked?" she repeated, squeezing his waist, thinking he had the thickest eyelashes of any man she had ever known. Those sexy bedroom eyes softened his rugged face just enough to be very appealing. His glower changed when she squeezed his waist again.

"Squeezed and poked and kissed," he amended.

She laughed, standing on tiptoe and curling her arm around his neck to kiss him lightly. "They'll go home early," she whispered in his ear, catching a whiff of his tantalizing after-shave.

"What other goodies are out in the Cadillac? They really have a knack. Spinach, carrots, and greens. The only other two things I detest to eat are—"

"Let me guess. Consommé. For all their special dinners they start with—"

He groaned. "I knew it! Dammit! I have thick, lean steaks in those grocery sacks. Crisp lettuce for salad. Nice potatoes."

"Your steaks will taste fine tomorrow."

"Yeah, and tonight I have to suffer through the type of dinner I was forced to eat when I was four years old! Greens were meant for billy goats—not humans! I can just guess what type of meat they brought. I'll go out and get the consommé and liver."

"You're saved from liver. It's fried chicken, and Aunt Sophie's recipe is yummy. I'll set the table," she said cheerfully. "Besides, greens are good for you."

"Yeah, so's buttermilk. Yuck! But fried chicken may make amends for all the rest."

During dinner Brink smiled and nodded politely while the two aunts chattered endlessly about mealtimes during the good old days when they'd been children at Saville.

Brink ate enough of everything to make the aunts happy. Hilary smiled at him each time he looked over at her, but they had little opportunity to converse. Mavis and Sophie were talkers, and they were delighted to have ensnared a new listener.

After dinner Brink insisted on cleaning up, and he sent the ladies to sit on the cool gallery. Actually he wanted a stiff drink and a chance to give his nerves some rest. He cleaned quickly, anxious to join Hilary. Otherwise he would have been tempted to slip away out the back door. He wondered if the sisters talked in their sleep. His ears rang already from their incessant chatter, and he knew that eventually they would broach the subject of Saville. He stared at the kitchen, focusing on the familiar old oak pedestal table where he had eaten as a child, then glancing over the high plate rail, displaying his grandmother's set of hand-painted china plates, each with a different bird.

"I came to make sure you hadn't skipped out," Hilary said, noticing the bottle of Scotch and his empty glass on the counter.

"The thought crossed my mind. But for you . . ."

"They like you. And you were a good sport about dinner."

"When will that damn sun go down?"

"In about an hour and a half," she said, slipping her arms around his waist. He smiled at her, feeling better as he lost himself in her green-eyed gaze. Unable to ignore the tension that danced between them, he lifted her chin with the knuckle of his forefinger and brushed her lips with his, hoping to make her want to be kissed as much as he wanted to kiss her.

Hilary closed her eyes; his lips were warm on hers, tantalizing as they touched the corner of her mouth, then he rained feathery kisses on her until she was burning with longing. Suddenly she could bear no more. She kissed him passionately, pulling his head closer, clinging to him tightly.

She knew he wanted her. His arms slipped around her waist and bound her tightly, his fingers splaying over her derriere, making her long for his caresses.

She moved her hips against him, relishing the feel of his solid length, knowing they should stop. "Brink, they'll wonder where we are. I'll look a fright."

"You'll never look a fright," he said softly, turning to lean back against the wall. He spread his legs apart and pulled her close between them. "This is the best feeling I've had in years. Don't make me stop just yet."

"How could I?" she whispered in return, sliding her arms around his neck and standing on tiptoe to kiss him again. His hands trailed down over her full breasts to her waist, then back to caress her breasts. He unbuttoned her shirt, slipping his hand beneath the cotton, pushing away her lacy bra to cup her soft fullness, flicking his thumb over her nipple, feeling it grow rigid. She moaned softly, the sound muffled by his mouth.

Brink crushed her in his arms, wanting to possess her softness. She was a flame in his arms, her potent kisses fueling the raging inferno of his need. He bent his head suddenly, pushing away cotton and lace to take her breast in his mouth and tease it lightly with his teeth. When he heard her moan of pleasure and felt her hips grind against him, his pulse pounded.

"Brink, we're not alone," she gasped.

He raised his head. His breathing was ragged, and he had to fight for control. He hurt from wanting her, but he released her, catching only a tantalizing glimpse of one rosy nipple before she adjusted her clothing and buttoned her blouse. Her face was flushed, her lips red, her hair slightly tousled; she looked sexy, enticing, and beautiful.

"Hilary, you're going to be the end of me," he said, his voice raspy.

"I'll go . . . back and talk to them."

She sounded subdued, and he wondered if she was also awed by the incredible electricity between them. Part of the attraction was physical, but it ran deeper. She was talented, fun, intelligent—and she was the most exciting woman he had ever known. He was falling in love with her with the speed of a falling star, but how deeply? There were numerous obstacles between them. He glanced around the kitchen. This house was a monumental source of trouble between them.

There was no doubt about it, she had thrown his life into absolute chaos! He poured himself another stiff drink of Scotch and braced himself to face her aunts. At least he could get out of seeing them the next day, having served his time tonight.

Mavis was espousing the virtues of home gardening when Brink joined them on the wide gallery with its handmade rail. Crickets chirped amid the fading light of dusk, and a cool evening breeze blew across the gallery. As he tuned Mavis out of his hearing, Brink basked in the peaceful setting. He hadn't realized how hectic his life had become with the constant demands of business and the frantic pace of city life. In contrast, Saville was very restful. The sprawling lawns were cool and soothing to his nerves.

Brink was watching a squirrel scamper through

the garden when he realized that Mavis had stopped talking and all three women were staring at him.

"Want to, Brink?" Hilary seemed amused.

"Want to what?" he asked.

"Stroll through the house. Mavis and Sophie will give us the grand tour, complete with a narration of what it was like when they were children."

The two ladies stood up, Mavis straightening slowly because her joints were stiff with arthritis.

Reluctantly Brink stood up to take Hilary's arm, sure that this was the longest day of his life!

In the front parlor Sophie said, "We had deep blue velvet drapes with gold trim. I thought they were the most elegant things I had ever seen. And there weren't windows on that side of the room. Those were added later."

"Is that right?" Brink asked, wondering who had made the changes in the house. "My grandfather must have put those in."

"He did. This marble for the fireplace was imported from France."

"It was? Grandpa never told me that."

"Some men don't remember things like that," Sophie said.

"True enough, but Grandpa was always interested in the house."

They'd only toured a few rooms on the first floor when Sophie noticed the time.

"We'd better be going, Sister," Mavis cautioned. "It's almost dark."

"Ladies, I'll be sure to return the dishes to you. And believe me, words can't express my feelings about the dinner you prepared," Brink said, taking their arms to walk them to the door.

"And I want to tell you, since we got to see each other tonight, there's no need in taking your time tomorrow—"

It was the last word he got in until they drove down the driveway.

"Dammit. I can boss two hundred men, run a corporation, and organize a charity golf match, but I can't get a word in edgewise with those two. They don't even stop talking to listen to each other! I am not going to visit them tomorrow. I'll call them and cancel. Wild horses can't drag me to that house for more spinach-and-carrot soufflé!"

Hilary linked her arm in his as they climbed the porch steps.

"Now admit it, Brink. The evening hasn't been all bad. You seemed to enjoy going through Saville with them."

"Well, honestly, I did. It was interesting to learn about the house. And you know, when it's restored, I think it should be decorated as it was originally. But it would be nice if they would just make a few, concise notes, instead of nonstop chatter!" He shrugged. "Hon, I'm sorry. I didn't mean to insult your aunts."

"Oh, that's all right. I knew how you felt about them before we met, and I can't expect you to become broad-minded overnight." She gazed off toward the setting sun. "Maybe I should go too."

"Don't be absurd. The evening is still young, and I *can* see to drive you home after dark. Way after dark!"

"Here I go—on dangerous ground again," she said, sitting down in a rocker. He moved his chair close, propped his feet on the porch railing, and sat back to enjoy the colorful sunset beside Hilary.

Hours later, Brink slid his feet onto the floor and reached out, tugging gently on her waist. "Come sit on my lap."

Eagerly she slipped into the warm security of his embrace. They kissed until she felt her control melting away. "Brink, I want to stop now. Our kisses are special, but they're potent and bewildering too. I can't get involved in a casual affair. I'm just not that type of person."

"I know that," he said tenderly. "I understand what you're saying to me, but that doesn't stop me from wanting you. I want to make love to you without reservations—"

"Without commitment?"

He stroked her cheek, thinking about his discovery during dinner. He was falling in love, but was he willing to throw his plans aside? Plans to remain single because of money he wanted to pour back into the business? Plans to remain a bachelor because of the freedom he enjoyed? "C'mon. I'll take you home to your water bed."

They linked arms and walked to the car. Brink drove her home, kissed her madly for a few minutes, and then left, telling her emphatically that he was not going to the Wakefield sisters' house tomorrow.

Warm sunshine spilled into the room the next morning as Hilary stretched and rubbed her face against the smooth pillow. Rolling over with a smile, she thought about Brink. She would spend all afternoon and evening with him. At first she had worried about losing her heart. She knew now that those worries were useless, because she had already lost it, completely and irrevocably. And she would just have to face the consequences as they came, because Brink Claiborn wasn't a man to settle down. He had made that clear from the beginning. And yet she hadn't been able to control her foolish heart around Brink. He was handsome, adorable, impossible—and probably hiding from her aunts right now.

The phone rang. Still smiling broadly, Hilary leisurely picked up the receiver. "Good morning," she said in a throaty voice, praying it was Brink.

"Hilary! Thank the Lord you're home!"

She lost her smile the moment she heard Sophie's heartrending sob. "Aunt Sophie, what is it?"

When she heard a wail in the background, Hilary became truly alarmed. "Aunt Sophie, calm down or I can't help!" she shouted, throwing back the sheets and leaping out of bed. "What's wrong?"

"Hilary, come quick. I think we've killed Mr. Claiborn!"

Eight

"You *what?*" Hilary shouted, yanking a shirt over her head.

"Hurry! This is dreadful! Dreadful!" Then the line went dead.

Hilary stared in consternation and fear. What had they done to Brink? Her aunts were so unpredictable! While she tugged on a pair of jeans she debated whether to call an ambulance or the sheriff or a doctor. Finally she called Dr. Whitley, the family doctor who'd delivered her.

"Dr. Whitley, this is Hilary. I'm sorry to disturb you, but we have an emergency."

"Honey, what's the prob—"

"Sophie and Mavis called and said they may have killed a man."

"How's that? What did you say?"

"They said they may have killed—"

"Oh, Lord. I knew they'd go too far someday. I'll go

see what's happened. Probably talked someone into a coma. I'm on my way now."

As she drove, Hilary could barely breathe. Brink! What could they have done to him? She shook with nervousness and fright. Brink was too strong and healthy for two little old ladies to kill. And if they *hadn't* killed him, when he came around, he might murder them! That she could imagine. She pressed the gas pedal and in seconds heard a siren. The police! Just what she needed. She swore as she pulled to the curb.

"Good morning. Oh, hi, Hilary. I didn't recognize your car. Going to a fire?"

"No, to a murder," she replied, glaring at Officer Jim Hollings, whom she had known for years.

He laughed. "That's a good one. Look, I'll just give you a warning ticket—"

"Jim, maybe I shouldn't tell you this, but Sophie just called me. She thinks she and Mavis may have killed a friend of mine. I don't know what they've done. I called Dr. Whitley, and he said he'd be right over."

"Mavis and Sophie hurt someone? C'mon, Hilary! Who're you kidding! They can't kill a spider!"

"It's Brink Claiborn."

"Claiborn? As in Saville?"

She nodded.

"I'll lead the way. Let's go."

He climbed on his motorcycle, turned on the siren, and pulled in front of her. They sped along faster than she had ever driven in her life. She ran up the walk, thankful to see Dr. Whitley's car in the drive.

"Thanks, Jim."

"I'll come inside and talk to them too."

"Will you have to report it?"

"Sorry. If there's a murder—"

"Oh, don't even say it!" she cried, and yanked open the front door to hear wailing.

Brink was stretched out on the floor. When she saw him move, Hilary nearly collapsed with relief. Dr. Whitley bent over him with a stethoscope in his hand.

Brink groaned, his lashes fluttered, and suddenly he began to curse, using language that Hilary was sure Mavis and Sophie had never heard.

"Oh, Lord, the Wakefield sisters have done it again!" Jim muttered. "See you around, Hilary."

"Don't go," she said, gripping his arm. "They may need you to protect them."

Brink shook his head, as if to clear it. He tried to focus on the man bending over him. Suddenly he arose with a roar, slugging Dr. Whitley. Then he spun around toward Mavis and Sophie. Both of them screamed and threw their arms around each other, cowering from him.

"Brink Claiborn, don't you dare hurt them!" Hilary shouted, dashing around the rose velvet settee.

"Don't hurt *them*!" he shouted. "Don't hurt *them*? They tried to kill me!" He swayed and staggered against the wall, swinging his arms. His speech was slurred, his steps shaky, until he fell forward and collapsed.

"Brink!" Hilary screamed this time.

"Dr. Whitley, get up! Brink passed out!"

"This crazy household! Mavis, you and Sophie al-

ways manage to conjure up the damnedest trouble."
The doctor rubbed his jaw as he knelt down to roll
Brink over. "What the hell—pardon me, ladies," Dr.
Whitley said. "What did you do to him?"

"Is he going to be all right?" Mavis asked.

"You tell me what in tarnation you did to him!
Then I'll tell you whether or not he'll be all right."

Mavis and Sophie burst into tears and hugged
each other.

"Dammit to hell, Hilary," Dr. Whitley snapped,
"can you get any information out of them?"

She stood up and walked over to take her aunts by
the arms. "Aunt Sophie. What did you do to Brink?"

"We'll go to prison! I've heard what they do to
people in prison. Unspeakable things!" she whispered, peering around Hilary at Jim.

"You're not going to prison unless he dies," Hilary
explained.

"Or unless he presses charges," Jim amended,
and both aunts burst into wails again.

"Jim . . ." Hilary said.

"Aw, gee. I'm sorry," he mumbled.

"Aunt Sophie, tell Dr. Whitley what you did to
Brink." At that moment Brink groaned. Both Dr.
Whitley and Jim backed away.

"He's coming around again, watch out!" Dr. Whitley said. "Sophie, for God's sake, tell me what you
did to the man before he slugs me again."

Mavis continued sobbing, but Sophie faced Hilary. "We just couldn't bear parting with Saville, and
we thought . . . we shouldn't have . . . I know how
foolish and terrible and ridiculous it was to think
we could get away with it."

"Get away with what?" Hilary cried. "What did you do?"

"We thought if we got him a little tipsy, we could get him to sign the agreement to sell us Saville."

Hilary closed her eyes while Dr. Whitley swore. Jim burst into guffaws, slapping his thigh until Dr. Whitley shot him a dark look.

"Tarnation! That wouldn't have been legal! You can't hold an intoxicated man to a contract!" Dr. Whitley said. "Now what did you give him, Mavis?"

"Poisoned his coffee. We laced it with Tom's bourbon—the vile liquor! I always told your uncle it was rotgut, no good for the system."

"Your Mr. Claiborn said it was as delicious as our turnip greens," Sophie added.

Hilary wished she were far, far away. "What will it do to him?" she asked Dr. Whitley.

"He's coming around again. Get back, everyone!" Dr. Whitley cried, scrambling to get away from the volatile patient.

Brink groaned, then bellowed and sat up, coming to his feet swiftly and weaving back and forth while he swore.

Mavis and Sophie screamed and fled from the room.

"Dammit to hell and back!" Brink shouted. "Turnip greens and soufflés and houses!"

"Man's gone mad about turnip greens," Dr. Whitley said, looking inquisitively at Hilary. "I need to find an antidote."

"Please hurry!" she pleaded.

"Go find your aunts. Ask them how much they gave him, a jigger or two, or what?"

Hilary ran.

"Stop!"

She froze, then turned to see Brink pointing his finger at her. "This shis all your malt—fault!"

"What did you do to him?" Jim asked her.

"Nothing!"

"Oh, yes, she did! Made me fall . . ." He started toward her, then stumbled forward, catching himself on a wing chair. "She made me fall . . . just plain fall . . ."

Dumbfounded, Hilary was staring at him just as intently as Jim and Dr. Whitley were.

"Go on, child. Ask Sophie how much they gave him," Dr. Whitley urged in a loud whisper.

"Damn Wakefields! They poisoned me!" Brink announced with great dignity, then his voice dropped back to a murmur. "And *she* made me fall in love!" With that, he passed out again, slumping over the wing chair.

"Call an ambulance!" Dr. Whitley said urgently to Jim, who disappeared in the direction of the kitchen, mumbling to himself about getting to the bottom of things.

"Hell, no!" Brink roared, stirring again, pushing himself up and waving his hand. "No ambulance."

"Son, we should get you to the emergency room," Dr. Whitley said from the kitchen doorway, "if only because the coffee is better down there than it is here," he confided. "I've had Sophie's coffee when it *wasn't* tainted!"

All the while Hilary had been watching Brink. He looked up, as if he'd noticed her. Then, slowly, as if it took great effort, he winked at her.

She fled to find Sophie.

"How much did you give him?" Hilary demanded of her aunt. Sophie merely sniffed and wiped her nose, hiding behind a handkerchief.

"Sophie, if you don't want charges brought against you, answer me!"

"We gave him half and half. Half alcohol and half coffee."

"Oh, Lordy!" Hilary ran back to tell Dr. Whitley as she heard the sirens approaching.

"No ambulance!" Brink yelled.

Hilary took his hand. "I'll ride with him," she told the doctor. "Be quiet, Brink."

He grinned at her. "Yes, honey."

"That's better," Dr. Whitley said with relief, looking at Hilary curiously. She knew rumors would be flying within the hour. "At any rate, we can all have a decent cup of coffee. Filmore's on the ambulance run this morning, and he always carries a thermos of Dottie's best brew."

"Jim, do you have to report this?"

The officer looked at Brink. "Depends on whether he presses charges."

"I doubt if he will," Hilary said quietly.

Jim shrugged. "Naw. No reports. But it sure was an interesting morning."

When the ambulance attendants came into the room and greeted Hilary and Dr. Whitley, Hilary wondered how many versions of the morning's events would sift through the town of Natchez.

On the way to the hospital, Brink opened his eyes and focused on Hilary. "What did they do to me?" His voice sounded more normal now.

"Several things," Dr. Whitley said.

Hilary brushed Brink's hair away from his forehead. "Is there any danger of lasting effects?" she asked Dr. Whitley.

"Nope. That 'poison' is probably about two hundred proof," he said, and chuckled. "Must be at least twenty years old. You're suffering from fusel oil—amyl alcohol. It's from inadequate care in distillation. Happens in the cheap stuff, and Tom sure as hell bought cheap booze. 'Course, Mavis used to pour his liquor right down the drain when she found it on the premises. It's a wonder this bottle lasted all these years."

"So you're telling me that I'm intoxicated." Brink mumbled with his eyes closed while he rubbed his temples.

"That's for sure!"

"Then why the hell am I in an ambulance!"

"To get you out of the house before you slugged me again! We'll check you over, make sure everything's okay. Then you're free to go."

"I slugged you?" Brink asked, still slightly dazed.

"Sure did, son. Mean right hook you have there. You a boxer?"

"Nope. I own a landfill company in Los Angeles."

"Ahh."

"They wanted to poison me?" he asked Hilary.

"I can't believe they would do that to you."

"I can," Dr. Whitley said. "Those two do the damnedest things. Remember when they thought old dead fish would help the garden, so they went down to the fish market—"

"I remember!" Hilary snapped.

"And what?" Brink asked with his eyes still closed. "What did they do? The Indians used to bury fish bones in the ground."

"Yeah, son," Dr. Whitley said, pouring more coffee.

"Fishbones *under* the ground makes good fertilizer. Mavis and Sophie bought a truckload of dead fish, and they had the guy dump it in their yard—on top of the ground." He took a sip and lowered his cup. "Do you know what a truckload of dead fish smells like on a warm spring afternoon?"

Hilary closed her eyes. "My aunts have done some strange things, but they've never resorted to violence! You drove them to it."

"*I* drove *them* to it!"

"Here we are. Lie down, son, and they'll carry you inside."

"Hell, I can walk." Brink jumped down and reached up to help Hilary, glowering at her. He helped Dr. Whitley climb down and thanked the drivers on the way into the emergency room.

An hour later Hilary and Brink emerged.

"I forgot! We don't have a car here." She paused and looked at him helplessly.

"Oh, that's just another one of those little things that makes this morning special," Brink said so pleasantly that she began to get nervous.

"I'll call a taxi."

"Relax, hon. I'll take care of it." He was back in minutes.

"Brink, I'm sorry."

He smiled. "It was nothing."

His good mood was suspect. She had a feeling she was dealing with an active volcano that was going to explode, not merely erupt. "I don't know what got into them. They have really never, ever done anything violent. Weird and strange but not violent. They're sorry."

"So am I, sweetie," he said with a smile.

"I was so worried about you! I just can't believe they would do such a thing. Brink, are you going to sue them?"

"Of course not, Hilary. A grown man doesn't sue two little old ladies just because they slip him a dose of twenty-year-old Scotch in his coffee."

"It was twenty-year-old bourbon."

"Whatever it was, their coffee killed the taste. I didn't recognize Scotch or bourbon."

"Oh, no! Look at that car! Let's go inside! Quick!"

"God! Are Mavis and Sophie here?" he asked, looking around.

"It's Izzy Throckmorton, from the newspaper."

"And that disturbs you?"

"You don't live here, dammit!"

"Don't be ridiculous. I'm not leaving now. We'll miss our cab."

A camera flashed, and she spun around. "Izzy! Brink, have you met Izzy Throckmorton?"

"What's the scoop, Mr. Claiborn?" Izzy asked as he shook hands with Brink. "Word has it that Miss Mavis and Miss Sophie tried to do you in with poison."

"Izzy, it wasn't poison!" Hilary snapped.

"The hell you say!" Brink glared at her. "It was their coffee!"

"That's all?" Izzy asked, sounding dubious and disappointed. "What are you doing in the hospital emergency room if it was just coffee?"

"Dr. Whitley said that we could get a better cup down here!" Hilary announced coolly.

"People don't check into the hospital just to get decent coffee!" Izzy said, scrutinizing her. "You two are hiding something. Why are you two together? A Claiborn and a Wakefield. Everyone knows about the feud the sisters have been having with you, Mr. Claiborn." Izzy looked back and forth between them in speculation, and Hilary gritted her teeth.

"Tell me the facts. I can just imagine my lead, 'Brink Claiborn mysteriously seen leaving hospital . . . with one of the Wakefields'!"

"Oh, Izzy!" Hilary snapped.

"Coffee? Is that all they gave you?"

"Here's our cab."

As Brink held the door open, Izzy stepped beside him. "Nothing except coffee?"

"Coffee and twenty-year-old bourbon," Brink shouted, then slammed the door.

As they drove away, Hilary saw the reflection of the camera's flash. "We'll probably be tomorrow's headlines," she said darkly.

"And whose fault is that?" Brink asked in that same quiet tone that reminded her of the calm before a storm.

"My car is at their house, and you probably shouldn't drive in your condition."

"The only condition I have now is a giant headache."

Hilary fell back against the seat and closed her eyes.

"Good morning, Miss Wakefield."

When Hilary opened her eyes, she recognized the cabdriver, Clarence Shipley. "Good morning, Clarence."

"Where to, folks? Say, are you Brink Claiborn? I heard 'em talking on my radio, and I thought it was just a rumor. Someone said Miss Mavis shot one of the Claiborns this morning. Lordy, Lordy, I'm sorry, Miss Wakefield."

"No one was shot. They were talking about Brink. Brink, meet Clarence Shipley. Clarence, this is Brink Claiborn."

"A Wakefield and a Claiborn in my cab at the same time! What's this old world coming to? Then there wasn't a shooting?"

"Not yet," Brink mumbled. "Can you take us to Saville? It's—"

"I know exactly where it is. I used to take your granddaddy back and forth."

"Do you know everybody in Natchez?" Brink whispered to Hilary.

Clarence glanced at Hilary in the mirror. "Were you two visiting someone in the hospital?"

"No, Clarence," Hilary said, wondering how many times she would have to explain. "Aunt Sophie served Brink her coffee laced with Uncle Tom's bourbon."

"Your Uncle Tom? He's been dead some twenty years now."

"So has his bourbon," Brink said, eliciting a frown from Hilary. He shrugged.

When the cab pulled up in front of Saville, she said, "I'll just go on home to—"

"No." Brink took her by the arm. Hilary took one look at the stubborn expression on his face and climbed out.

While he paid Clarence she waited on the gallery. He came up the steps without acknowledging her, unlocked the door, opened it, and waited for her to go inside. Then Hilary braced herself for the explosion.

"Dammit, dammit, dammit!"

"Don't shout at me. I can't help what they did, and I told you I was sorry!"

"This is your confounded fault! I could just shake you."

"My fault? How on earth can you say it's my fault, Brink Claiborn? The bourbon must have tainted your brain!"

"I wish I had never heard the name Wakefield. I wish I'd let you swish your pretty little fanny right across that mined demolition site. If the charges had gone off, we'd have probably all been safer than we are right here in the same town with dear little Aunties Sophie and Mavis." He lunged toward her.

Hilary backed up. "Brink, are you all right?"

"Well, hell, no, I'm not all right! If I was all right, would I be shouting at you? Every bit of this is your fault, Hilary Wakefield!"

She backed around the sofa, and he followed. "I think you're still a little disoriented, Brink. Sit down and let me call Dr. Whitley."

"I'm not disoriented," he snapped. "I feel like the Jolly Green Giant is doing a tap dance on my head. Everything is a little woozy. I don't think I want to see food again in this lifetime, and I may be a teetotaler for the rest of my life! But I am not disoriented." As he spoke, his voice lowered, reflecting the calm control that she knew meant trouble.

"Stop chasing me!" Hilary snapped, shaking a finger at him.

"This whole thing is your fault!"

"And stop telling me that when it's not true!" she exclaimed, her voice rising in anger. "Don't you bully me! I didn't do a damn thing!"

"If it weren't for you, I wouldn't be here. If it weren't for you, I wouldn't be mixed up with any Wakefields! If it weren't for you, I wouldn't be an addlepated jackass who can't keep my mind on anything for more than ten minutes straight! If it weren't for you, I wouldn't be in love, and love doesn't fit in with my schedule!"

She stopped walking backward around the sofa and let him catch up with her. "You're in love?"

"Yes, dammit!"

"You don't act like it."

"I'm not happy about it. You're complicating my life, and your relatives are shredding my nerves. They tried to do me in this morning. And no one is going to arrest them—"

"Arrest them!"

"That's what usually happens when someone tries to commit murder."

"Twenty-year-old bourbon isn't lethal."

"You didn't drink it!"

"Let's go back to the part about your being in love."

As he stared at her, she saw the change come over him. His fury vanished, giving way to a look of hungry desire that made her want to melt. She rushed into his arms as he reached for her, and all anger and fear disappeared.

Her heart hammered violently as she clung to him. "I was so worried about you," she whispered between kisses.

"I'm sorry I shouted. You really do bring out something atavistic in me."

"I'm not crying because you shouted at me. I knew you didn't really mean it. I'm crying because I'm relieved. I was so scared. Aunt Sophie called and said they had killed you—"

"Hilary, I've heard enough about your aunts." He looked at her a moment, then bent his head to kiss her, and she didn't say another word.

"I love you, and I don't know what I'm going to do about it," he murmured against her throat.

She held him tighter, placing her lips on his, stopping his words. He scooped her into his arms and carried her to the sofa where he sat down and pulled her close, cradling her head against his shoulder. Her slender legs stretched out on the cushions while he bent over her and kissed her.

His fingers unfastened the buttons on her blouse, pushed away the fabric, and opened the catch on her bra. His big hand cupped her breast, and he lowered his head to take her nipple into his mouth, teasing her. Hilary closed her eyes and let her hands drift over him, exploring. She wanted the barrier of clothing gone, yet still felt hesitant.

Sensing her reluctance, he shifted away, took a deep breath, then stood up. "I'd better take you home."

"Your car is at Aunt Sophie's."

"Oh, damn."

When Brink left the room to call a cab, Hilary wondered why he had stopped kissing her and moved off the sofa so abruptly.

"I'll see you this afternoon, Hilary," he said as he leaned down to close the door to the taxi.

To her relief, she didn't know the cabdriver and was able to ride home in silence. Her nerves were shattered, yet she felt as if she were walking one foot above the ground. Brink loved her. Although he didn't want to, and he didn't know how to cope with his feelings, he had admitted that he loved her.

And she loved him, absolutely. She was more and more sure each time she was with him, even during the fracas that day, even during his angry tirade. Why did they have such an explosive effect on each other?

She spent the next two hours trying to soothe her aunts, obtaining a prescription for their nerves from Dr. Whitley and calling Sam Jarvis, the family lawyer.

Finally at home, she dressed carefully for her date with Brink, pulling on blue shorts and a blue shirt and sandals.

When he opened the door, she noticed the flare of pleasure in his eyes.

"Wow," he said softly. "Come inside. Maybe we'll cancel the plans for the afternoon and just stay here."

"We'd better stick to the original plans," she said, stepping inside. "How's your head?"

"Still there. Hard as ever," he said. His voice became softer, and he pulled her into his arms. "Hi."

When he bent his head to kiss her, she clung to him, her heart thudding with eagerness. Each rapturous kiss reminded Hilary that Brink was falling in love with her, just as she was falling in love with him.

It was a gloriously sunny day. They rode down the Mississippi on a boat Brink had rented. When they discovered a cluster of oak trees, their limbs draped with graceful moss, Brink dragged the boat ashore. Reclining on the riverbank, they talked about their hopes and fears, their dreams. Hilary realized that Brink was deeply ambitious, wanting to franchise his business. By the time they returned to the dock at Natchez-Under-the-Hill, the sun was low in the sky, sending orange rays across the river. Brink held her hand as they walked ashore.

"Ever swim in the Mississippi?"

She laughed. "I wasn't supposed to, but I did. Just a little way out, and I held on to the branch of a willow tree because I was told the currents are deep and strong."

"They are, but I've been in it too. It's muddy as hell. Should we try a fish dinner down here by the river?" he asked, pointing to a restaurant with tables on a rustic porch.

"Sure. Whatever you'd like. You're the visitor in this town."

When they were seated at a wooden table covered by a red-checked tablecloth, they ordered local specialties. Over salty margaritas he said, "I think we need to put a little distance between this morning and our future together. Are your aunts all right?"

"They are terrified that you'll try to put them in prison."

"I would never do such a thing, but I'm not going to visit them again on this trip."

"That's fine. In turn, they have promised never again under any circumstances to resort to violence. Dr. Whitley wrote them a prescription for tranquilizers."

Brink smiled, then laughed and shook his head. "Which one slipped me the Mickey Finn? Sophie, probably."

"Of course. Mavis can't stand to hurt anything."

They dined on fried catfish and hush puppies as they watched tourists board the *Natchez Belle*. The charming old boat churned away from the landing, banjo music floating on air as the big paddle wheel stirred the water to a froth.

After dinner they ambled up Silver Street, past the long, narrow buildings that now held shops and an inn but once had been dens of vice. When they reached the top of the yellow-brown bluffs, they turned south and strolled down the street to a grassy area near Rosalie. They cuddled together on a bench overlooking the river.

Brink held her close to his side as they discussed the economy in Natchez. Finally he said, "I'm going to see if I can buy a landfill company here."

Nine

Hilary stared at Brink as if he had dropped a bomb. "You're moving from Los Angeles to Natchez?"

"Not year-round. But I've been thinking about it. I want to see more of you. A lot more."

She couldn't believe her ears. "Why?"

He smiled a lazy smile. The sensuous glimmer in his eyes sent a tingle coursing through her. "You know why," he said in a voice so powerful, it seemed to flow around her like the river around the rocks, enveloping her in a current that swept her along. "We need to get to know each other."

He lifted her hand to brush his lips across her knuckles. The faint touches scalded her senses. "I want you, Hilary. Someday you'll be mine. I'm going to love you hour after hour." The look in his eyes was as devastating as his words.

"Besides," he continued, "it's peaceful here. I'm glad to be back. Life in Los Angeles is a lot more hectic. I'd forgotten what it's like here."

Hilary detected a wistful note in his voice. She could understand how Natchez would be more relaxing, but there was something very forceful and dynamic about Brink that made it difficult to picture him settling down in Natchez. And she couldn't imagine such a thing, just to be with her! The mere thought made her pulse dance.

"If I can find the right business here, find someone eager to sell something solid and reputable, then I can work in Natchez as well as in Los Angeles."

"I'll have to see it to believe it."

"You will," he said firmly. "When I make up my mind, I stick with my decision. And when I want something," he said, looking at her intently, "I go after it."

"How will you get back and forth?"

"I'll admit that it's a problem without a direct flight, but I can manage."

She was stunned at his announcement. Suddenly all the implications swirled in her mind.

Brink stood up and pulled her to her feet. "I think it's time to take you home where we can really be alone."

When they arrived at her house, they sat on her patio and talked, mesmerized by the churning waters of the Mississippi. Hours later, when he kissed her long and hard and bid her good night, she realized the restraint he was using.

They spent Sunday together, until he had to leave. It wasn't until he was gone that she picked up the Sunday paper and remembered Izzy Throckmorton. She braced herself for wild headlines, but to her relief, there was only a brief story on page four, which told how Brink Claiborn, grandson of Carlton

Claiborn, had been treated and released for a stomach upset after visiting Mavis and Sophie Wakefield. And thankfully, there were no pictures.

In the late afternoon Hilary visited her aunts. The ladies were still in shock, horrified over what they had done. In spite of Hilary's strong assurances, they wanted to make it up to Brink next time he came to town.

Hilary spent the next week in a daze. Her usual efficiency vanished, because her mind was preoccupied with Brink. Separated from his powerful presence, she missed him all the more.

He called every night, and they talked for hours each time. On Wednesday morning a florist appeared at Hilary's house before she left for work. He handed her a basket of two dozen red roses. Smiling, she pulled out the card: "In spite of spinach, carrots, coffee, and bourbon, I love you. Brink."

Delighted, she took a deep whiff of the roses, pulled one long-stemmed rose out of the bouquet, and placed it in a separate bud vase by her bed. As soon as she thought he would be home from work, she called him and thanked him.

That weekend Brink couldn't get away, but on the next one he came to Natchez, arriving on Saturday afternoon. When Hilary opened her door, she flew straight into his outstretched arms. He looked wonderful in herringbone slacks, a white casual shirt open at the throat, and black lizard-skin loafers. He held her away and explained, "I'd like to see Grandpa. Want to come with me?"

"Of course. That's really grand of you."

"You make me sound as if I neglect him. Hilary, I

can't take him to Los Angeles, and if he were able, he wouldn't want to go."

"I didn't say anything about taking him to Los Angeles! It's just that sometimes, Brink, you seem far more interested in material things than in people."

He frowned for a second, then smiled. "I'm not going to get into an argument. Not tonight, of all times. *Things* are important, too, Hilary. Look at the things in the world that have been preserved through history that are so important to people— Stonehenge, the Great Pyramids. If Mt. Vernon had been left to the Wakefields, it might not be here today," he said mildly.

"That's absurd! Wakefields aren't in the business of destruction. You just give things more priority than people."

He arched his brows and studied her solemnly. "We won't argue about which you put first."

"I saw Carlton on Wednesday, for about an hour."

"You're still visiting Grandpa?" He squeezed her hand, lacing his fingers through hers. "You're sweet, you know?"

"I'll remind you of that the next time you start shouting at me."

"I'd tell anyone else I'm all bark and no bite," he said in a raspy voice that made her gasp, "but I can't with you, because I *do* want to bite." He leaned down to kiss her.

Finally he released her and said, "We'd better go if I'm going to visit Grandpa. He'll be asleep for the night soon."

That night Brink treated her to her favorite dish. They dined on steaming jambalaya by candlelight in an old inn overlooking the river. Afterward they went back to her house to relax on the patio. She settled into the lawn chair, curling her legs beneath her, smoothing the skirt of her yellow crepe-de-chine sleeveless dress down over her legs. Millions of stars twinkled above, but they couldn't match the sparkle she felt deep inside when she was around Brink. The moon was a white circle in the sky, casting a silvery tint upon the earth, revealing Brink's face clearly. Hilary yearned to touch and kiss him.

As Brink spoke, he removed pins from her hair until it was down, curling softly around her shoulders.

His fingers moved back and forth on her bare shoulder and across the nape of her neck. He caressed her for over an hour, seemingly oblivious to touching her, but she was far from oblivious. Each stroke added to the fires building within her. His long legs were stretched in front of him, crossed at the ankles. Her gaze drifted down as she wondered how he looked beneath the slacks, how it would feel to lay beside him, his length pressed against her.

"I took the contract in spite of the guy," he was saying. "It only leaves one week between jobs. You probably don't agree."

She heard something about agreeing, and he looked at her expectantly. She blinked, then shrugged. "I'm afraid you lost me there."

He laughed and caught her wrist lightly, pulling her closer.

She moved to his lap without urging, her arms going around his neck as he pulled her close. "I thought we'd never get around to this!" she murmured as he kissed her throat beneath her ear, making her ache for his lips on hers. "Brink—"

He kissed her on the mouth, and passion burst inside her, sending sparks dancing through her veins. She pressed against him, wanting him as she had never dreamed it was possible to want a man, wanting to give herself totally to him because she loved him.

His fingers fumbled over the decorative pearl buttons that ran from the high neck of her dress down to her waist. "How the hell do these unbutton?" he murmured, letting his hand drift over her curves, feeling his heart pound violently. He wanted her. His entire body ached and throbbed with need for her. He was determined to demolish every last vestige of her restraint.

"It zips down the back," she whispered, covering his throat with light kisses that made him groan softly. He stood, scooped her into his arms easily, and carried her through the open glass doors to her bedroom.

Moonlight bathed her face so that he could see the languorous expression in her half-closed eyes, her parted lips. He thought of the nights he had restrained himself from making love to her. Tonight he wanted her. He wanted to make her his forever, to bind her to him. He wanted to look and taste and touch this woman who offered such a sensual promise, yet seemed unaware of her power.

He turned her around, kissing the nape of her neck as his big fingers tugged the zipper below her waist. She was wearing only a brief, lacy bra, bikini panties, a garter belt, and stockings. He pushed the dress off her shoulders, letting it fall and billow around her ankles. As she stepped out of it, he slipped his arm around her, turning her to face him.

He looked at her, the roaring in his ears drowning out the sound of his breathing. She was so lovely. Forcing himself to go slowly, he teased her throat with light kisses.

Her fingers were feathery, drifting over him, tugging at his buttons and belt. Although her touch was gentle, it inflamed his desire, forcing him to struggle for control. He peeled away the bits of lace and the stockings, momentarily holding her away from him to drink in the sight of her pale, slender body, her full breasts and dusky nipples.

And then his clothes were gone, and Hilary studied him eagerly. She would always remember the sight and feel of Brink's body, his broad chest with a mat of dark, curly hair that tapered to a narrow line to his navel, his slim hips, his throbbing manhood, which made her reach for him.

He kissed her, his voice raspy as her fingers wound in his hair. His thumbs drew circles around the twin peaks of her breasts, then he took them in his mouth, first one, then the other, teasing her, hearing her soft moans of pleasure, caressing her until she was quivering with need and crying out for him.

Her hands trailed over him with an eagerness that revealed her desperate desire. Together they sank to the floor. He knelt over her to kiss her from her throat to her knees. Each time she gasped, his pulse jumped a notch.

"Honey, I'll protect you," he said.

"Brink," she whispered, holding out her arms. She needed this virile man, his manhood throbbing with desire. She ached for him, knowing this was right.

Moonlight splashed over his corded muscles. His breathing was ragged as he lowered his weight over her. Trying to go slowly, he thrust into her softness and heard her muffled cry. When she wrapped her arms around him, he kissed her deeply.

"Put your legs around me," he commanded, kissing her throat, trying to hold back, wanting to make it good for her.

Hilary felt impaled, filled with him. She surged each time he moved, thrusting slowly, until ecstasy approached. Her hips moved, meeting his rhythm until she was lost, and rapturous sensations washed over her, carrying her to the brink of passion. Release burst when she heard his hoarse whisper.

"Hilary, now!"

She cried out; then her cry was gone because his mouth was over hers, kissing her, making her forget that the world existed. There was only Hilary and Brink, and they were one.

His weight covered her, and for endless moments they lay locked in each other's arms. "I love you, Hilary, more than you can imagine. You're mine," he drawled in a husky voice. "All mine, only mine, forever mine."

He rolled away, pulling her with him, fitting her against his side as he propped his head on his hand, elbow bent, to look down at her. "At this moment I feel as if I own the world," he whispered, his gaze drifting down the length of her while she ran her forefinger along his strong jaw.

"I'm in paradise," she whispered.

"Let's try to make it last," he said, suddenly serious. "Promise?"

"Yes," she answered as solemnly, feeling a surge of joy because he was making a commitment. "I'll try if you will."

"We'll make it last, honey." He twisted and fumbled with his discarded clothing. She heard keys jingle, and then he rolled back over to face her again. "I want you forever—as long as we both shall live. That's the way I think they put it." He held out a ring. "Will you marry me?"

Ten

"Brink! Good grief, you are full of surprises!" Hilary sat up and faced him. "Marry?"

"Marry."

They searched each other's eyes, and she threw her arms around his neck. "Damn right, I will!" she cried, knocking him flat. His arms banded around her instantly, pulling her down on top of him.

"That's one of the things I like about you—your enthusiasm. I like the way you respond so quickly when I reach for you."

"Where did that ring go?"

He chuckled and opened his fist. "Give me your hand." He slipped the ring on her finger, his smile vanishing as he looked up at her. "I'm stubborn, hot-tempered, inconsiderate, and whatever else you called me. You'll put up with all that? I can't promise to reform."

"I'll take you just the way you are," she said happily, full of joy. At the moment their differences were negligible. "I'll take you just like this, all muscle and trim waist, and lean, sexy legs," she said, wiggling slowly and provocatively against him.

He groaned, tightened his arm around her waist, and rolled her over. Once again she had aroused him, filling him with hot desire. He gazed down at her hungrily, his passion as blatant as it had been an hour before. Then he lowered his head to kiss her.

An hour later she lay in his arms studying her ring, catching a shaft of moonlight that twinkled and sparkled in the huge diamond.

"I hope you didn't hock everything you own to get this for me. It's enormous!"

"I don't want you to forget me. I want you to notice it constantly."

She laughed softly. "Forget you? That's a knee slapper! I wish you had told me you were getting this serious. I've been expecting you to vanish right out of my life as suddenly as you came into it."

"You came into mine, love, sashaying your enticing little bottom right over a field of dynamite! And how in sweet hell could you possibly think I'd vanish when I'm getting ready to buy a landfill company here? I travel thousands of miles, halfway across the United States, to be with you."

"I'm not a mind reader, and you're a mysterious male. I don't know what you're thinking."

"You don't, huh?" he asked, lowering his hand.

"Brink!"

"You do know what I'm thinking," he said, rolling over to smile at her. They both laughed, then he bent his head to kiss her breast. "That felt nice. And was a good idea." He raised his head. "Can we get married soon?"

"Soon enough, but we'll want to invite all our relatives and friends. It'll take a little time to plan the wedding."

"Okay, but I would prefer tomorrow."

"Brink, what about your businesses? Can you buy a company here and then be so far away from it part of the year? And what about your business in Los Angeles? Won't they both go to pot?"

"Don't worry," he answered. "I have an excellent man in charge in Los Angeles—the one you thought was the brains of the business."

"Just a reasonable mistake. You looked as if you had been grubbing in the dirt for a year!"

He grinned and continued, "And I'll get a reliable person to handle things here. I can set up various arrangements, offer them a percentage of the business, some incentive. There are qualified workers out here; I'll just have to find one in this area." He ran his fingers through her hair, stroking her throat. "The real question is, can you leave your shop for half of the year?"

"I'll have to find a job for the other half in Los Angeles."

"Not necessarily. I can afford to let you loaf."

"I can't afford it! I want to work. I can probably find a job in an antique shop."

"Or I can open one for you."

"I can't let you do that!"

"Of course you can. You can pay me back out of the profits from the store. It'll be another investment for Claiborn Industries. How's that sound?"

"You don't even know if I'm any good at the antique business!"

"Are you in the red or the black?"

"The black."

"The pleased tone in your voice makes me think you are very much in the black."

"We've done nicely."

"I have a hunch that I'm getting a shrewd little businesswoman in the family. A little bonus I didn't expect!" He trailed kisses across her stomach, then raised his head to look at her. "I want you in my arms every night and every morning, and I want you all to myself for a long honeymoon. You can pick any place you'd like to go in the whole world."

"Brink, I have some money saved."

"Do you now?" he asked, his lips between her breasts.

"Mmm, yes. We . . . Brink, don't you . . . want to talk?"

He didn't answer, but she didn't care. Once again she was lost to his lovemaking, filled with rapture over the night, over Brink's love and his proposal.

When the first rays of dawn lit the horizon, they watched them from a chaise on her patio.

"Maybe we'd better go inside," she said, watching a boat cruise down the river.

"Why?" he asked in a deep voice.

She crossed her arms protectively. "Well, there's a whole boat full of people going past. . . ."

"They can't see you. There are miles between us."

"I'm modest and shy."

"Yeah, I know!" he said dryly, chuckling with satisfaction.

"I feel as if they can see us."

He sighed. "Okay, whatever the lady wants." He picked her up and carried her inside to the water bed, where they lingered until the middle of the afternoon.

"Brink, this seems sort of decadent. Shouldn't we eat or something?" she asked, sitting up to look at him. She trailed her fingers over his chest, wondering at the marvels of his body.

"The 'something' sounds best to me!"

"I mean it. Your stomach keeps growling."

He laughed and nudged her off the bed. "That's your delicate stomach, sweetie. I guess it's time to nourish that delectable body of yours," he said, propping himself up to watch her move around the room.

"If you don't quit staring at me like that, we won't get a chance to eat!"

"I'm just looking," he said innocently.

"It's the *way* you're looking."

He laughed and swung his feet out of bed.

"Oh, no, Brink! I know that gleam in your eyes. We're going to dress and eat!"

His arm snaked out and caught her around the waist, and he pulled her to him. "You can go bathe in a minute. Do you know how much I love you?"

She shook her head, her voice growing soft. "Tell me. Tell me over and over forever."

"I love you so much," he said briskly, "that I'm going to become a relative of Miss Mavis and Miss Sophie. Now, hon, that is love beyond all great loves in history!"

"You poor soul!"

"Poor soul is right! I'm lucky to be alive to propose, no thanks to them."

"I don't want to hear about that morning for the rest of my life, Brink Claiborn!"

"You've got a deal there. But you may want to tell them I'm allergic to spinach and greens."

"Deal!"

"And one more thing. As I recall, I've won a bet that requires you to spend a week in Los Angeles."

"That isn't necessary now that we're getting married," she said sweetly, slipping out of his grasp.

"That's just like a woman! To cheat on a bet!"

She went to shower, and when she came out, he was studying her paintings and sketches. He held one in his large hands. "When did you do this?"

It was the pencil sketch she had done of him during the past week, while he had been away in Los Angeles. "This week. It's just a sketch."

"It's damn good. Hilary, you can't go on ignoring your talent."

"Would you want me painting night and day when we're married?"

"Of course not, but there's a happy medium. You don't have to be Matisse to earn a living at it, achieve something with it, share it with others. You have a unique gift."

"Mister, you are biased. I'm merely competent," she answered flippantly.

"You're a hell of a lot more than competent. What kind of grades did you get in art in college?"

She grinned. "Point in your favor."

He smiled. "Come on. What kind of grades?"

"Maybe pretty good ones."

"Uh-huh. Any shows?"

"A few. Brink, I'm starving! I have to eat."

"Any ribbons or awards?" he persisted, catching her around the waist and turning her to face him.

"A few, but—"

"But nothing. I can't imagine selling antiques if I could draw and paint the way you do."

"Well, that's just one of my little quirks you're

going to have to learn to live with. Think you can?" she asked lightly, but she waited without taking a breath until he nodded.

"You bet I can! It's your decision when it gets right down to it."

"I'm glad to hear you admit that."

"It seems such a colossal waste. Don't you enjoy painting?"

"Oh, of course I do!"

He tilted his head to study her intently. "Then what is really holding you back?"

She paused and stared beyond him. He had to lean closer to hear her quiet answer. "I suppose when it comes right down to it, I'm scared," she answered, finally looking him in the eye. "Brink, I'm afraid I'm not good enough. There are so many talented artists out there."

"That's true of every field, honey. There are some other fine antique stores in this town, yet yours does well."

"That's different, somehow. I pour a little more of myself into each of my drawings. It's so personal; the thought of failure terrifies me."

He put his arms around her. "I can't imagine a woman who will drive over explosives being terrified of failure. Particularly when you're so talented."

Running her fingers over his broad shoulder, down to the mat of hair on his chest, she sobered, thinking about all he had said. "It's not just a matter of talent. It's hard work. If I work ninety hours at the store, I get to eat. I can work ninety hours at painting and not earn a dime." It was good to tell someone, although she thought Brink had a biased viewpoint about her talent. "I came out of college expecting to go into something else. All I ever heard all my life was that I wouldn't be able to earn a living as an artist."

"Then why did you major in it?"

"Well, some dreams die slowly. If I had it to do over, I'd change my major. Chalk that one up to youth."

"What would you major in now?"

"Business. I've thought about getting an M.B.A."

"You mean, going back to school full-time?"

"No! Just taking night courses. It wouldn't take forever."

"Hell's bells! Instead of sacrificing your evenings to work on an M.B.A., why don't you spend them painting?"

She wiggled her fingers at him. "I think this ring means I'm going to spend them with you."

He grinned and caught her hand to kiss it. "I think you're right."

She stood on tiptoe and lost herself in his embrace, until she slipped out of his grasp. "I'll have something delicious for you when you're through showering."

They ate bacon and eggs and buttered toast. Over a cup of steaming coffee, Brink gazed at her solemnly. "Honey, when I get a business here, there's something we need to discuss."

"This sounds important."

"It is. You have a home here. I have a home here, Saville. Where are we going to live?"

"I know how you love Saville, Brink. It'll be fine."

"But you don't like old houses. I remember you swore you'd never live in one again."

"I don't care, as long as I'm with you. It's a beautiful old home. And we'll be living in Los Angeles for part of the year."

He grinned. "So all that big temper tantrum of yours about my Los Angeles house being an unlivable museum—"

"Brink, there's something I want you to know. I never lose my temper. Absolutely never! Except with you."

"Somehow I can believe that, because you make me do things I don't intend to do."

She carried her plate to the sink and came back to him, resting her hand on his shoulder. "Like marriage?"

He pushed back his chair and pulled her down on his lap. "Nope. I know what I'm doing, and I'm ten feet above the ground with happiness today."

She leaned down and kissed his cheek.

"I have some other plans for Saville. It should be a museum that people can enjoy. Besides, I can't imagine you home alone in that huge house. I've got an idea."

"And what's this red-hot idea of yours?" she asked, kissing him again.

The excited glimmer in his eyes piqued her curiosity. "You have a gorgeous location but a very small house. Why don't we tear down your house and rebuild?"

"That's expensive."

"Not really. And you can design the house— with an architect, of course. Do you like that idea?"

"Of course I love the idea!"

"Settled. On to the next problem."

"Well, there's something we have to do."

"Uh-oh. I know that tone of voice oh, so well." He watched as she slid off his lap and crossed the room to put away the toaster. "What is it, honey?" he asked.

"We have to go tell Mavis and Sophie about our plans."

"Can't you do it without me?"

"No!" She came across the kitchen to sit down facing him. "You have to go too. Brink, you have to talk to them sooner or later."

"How about later? Like five years from now?"

"You want a wedding five years from now?"

"Okay, okay."

"When I go to work tomorrow, we'll either have to keep our engagement a secret or be ready for everyone in town to know. And my aunts should hear the news before everyone else in town finds out. It would hurt their feelings terribly."

"Hilary, do you realize they tried to hurt far more than just my feelings?" He winked at her. "Let me get into a suit of armor and strap on a six-shooter, then I'll go with you."

She wrinkled her nose at him playfully. "That was so odd for them. They can't even bear to kill flies."

"You'll never convince me. And I hope we're not going to celebrate the announcement with Uncle Tom's bourbon."

"Of course not!" she said, disappearing into the bathroom.

Brink's heart beat swiftly with happiness. He adored Hilary. Her aunts were a deluxe pain in the ass, but it was a package deal. Hilary couldn't help being born a Wakefield, no more than she could control the actions of her dear, eccentric aunts.

Twenty minutes later, Hilary emerged in a pale blue cotton skirt and white blouse and stockings.

"You're dressed up," he said, giving her an appreciative appraisal.

"This is a special occasion. It will be the first time I get to announce my engagement, and I want to look nice for it. Will you button me, please? These are hard to fasten because they're—"

He slipped his hands beneath the blouse, cupping her breasts.

"Brink!" She turned around. "Maybe I'd better struggle with my own buttons if we want to get there."

"Come back here," he said softly. "I'll keep my hands busy with buttons, but I just couldn't resist. I like the blue underwear."

"Buttons, mister."

"Sure, sure. Just one more little—"

"Brink!"

She scooted away, finished dressing, and then picked up the phone to call her aunts.

"Aunt Sophie," she said into the phone while Brink kissed her nape. "Mmm. Brink is here." She twisted around to look at him and covered the mouthpiece of the phone. "I can't think with you doing that!"

He grinned devilishly, crossing his arms. "Aunt Sophie, we're coming over to see you."

The screech that followed her announcement made Hilary hold the phone away from her ear and blush with embarrassment. Brink shook his head, equally bewildered.

"Aunt Sophie, listen to me! He's not bringing the law after you! We just want to come visit. Just the two of us. No, don't cook anything. Don't go to any trouble."

"For Lord's sake, no!" Brink snorted in disgust as he left the room. She stared at the empty doorway.

"We'll see you in about twenty minutes. And don't worry. Brink is very nice, and he won't hurt you."

He leaned around the corner of the doorway as she replaced the receiver. "I heard that. Don't make rash promises for me."

"You wouldn't hit two little helpless ladies!"

"Only in self-defense," he snapped, and then held out his arms and grinned. "Let's get going, before I have a chance to change my mind!"

The closer they came to the Wakefield house, the more silent Brink became.

"Brink, honey, we don't have to stay long. Stop looking as if you are going to have to crawl into the ring with Sugar Ray Leonard."

"I would prefer that, Hilary, if you want to know the truth."

"My aunts are really harmless."

"Yeah, sure. And the sky is green today."

"How about an August wedding?"

"That long?"

"We have a lot of arrangements to make."

"Whatever the lady wants. Can you make it August first?"

"How about the twentieth? It's a Sunday."

"Absolutely wonderful!" he said quickly, excitement coursing through him at the thought of having Hilary to himself all the time.

When they turned into the narrow driveway, Hilary placed her hand on his arm. "You know, when I came home from California, I took a good look at this house."

"And?"

"You were right. It's run-down, but that doesn't mean it can't be maintained properly. I'm going to hire a maid to clean once a week, and I'll make sure repairs and painting are done when they're needed. You know, I just never noticed. Look over there, Brink!" She waved her hand toward the panorama of colorful azaleas. "How can you look at cobwebs when there are all these gorgeous flowers to see?"

"Because I'm concerned about safety. A hell of a lot of good these azaleas will do if the house falls in because of termites!"

"Aunt Sophie wears bifocals, and Aunt Mavis wears trifocals. I don't think they see cobwebs and cracks and dust."

"That doesn't mean those things won't ruin the house, Hilary. That's what's important."

"There you go, getting carried away with *things* again!"

"And there you go, losing your common sense! It isn't as if I'm putting them out of their house and onto the street. I just don't want them living in my house!"

"Are we fighting?"

He grinned. "Hell, no! I have big plans for tonight. Want me to tell you about them?" he asked in a softer voice.

She winked at him and gave him a light kiss. "Tell me later, or we might not get out of this car."

"I'm sure we can find some privacy behind an azalea bush—"

"Brink!"

"All right, all right."

When they entered through the back door, Brink grew noticeably tense.

"Yoo hoo! We're here," Hilary called when she stepped into the kitchen.

There was no answer. She took Brink's hand and led him down the wide central hallway. "Yoo hoo! Aunt Mavis? Aunt Sophie?"

"Hilary—"

"Don't worry! They're here. They're probably embarrassed."

"Maybe they've run away from home."

"Don't be absurd! Aunt Sophie, where are you?"

"Here," came a faint answer.

"See, I told you," Hilary whispered to Brink. "They're in the living room."

The two aunts sat close together on the rose sofa, holding hands. They flinched when Brink entered the room.

"We apologize, Mr. Claiborn," Sophie said. Both women nodded and began to dab at their eyes.

He looked helplessly at Hilary and shook his head, mouthing, "I told you so!"

"Aunt Sophie, Aunt Mavis, please don't cry," Hilary pleaded. "It makes men nervous."

The women sniffed and coughed, firming their lips, dabbing at their red eyes, and glaring at Brink.

"Sit down, Brink," Hilary urged.

"It's all right, ladies," he said, feeling uncomfortable. The Wakefield sisters made him nervous. There was something unpredictable about them. "Bygones are bygones," he said, trying to force some cheer into his voice, "and we'll forget about what happened." Brink wanted to get the hell out of the place, but Hilary sat down, as if she were settling in for the day. He wondered what he had gotten himself into, proposing to the niece of two of the battiest women he had ever encountered. The Wakefields. His better half.

Then Hilary crossed her slender, tanned legs, shook her fall of golden hair away from her face, smiled at him with rosy lips, and he knew what he had gotten himself into. He thanked heaven he had found her. Aunts be hanged. He had learned how to deal with landfill and demolition. He could learn to tolerate the senior Wakefields!

Hilary beamed at him, then leaned forward. "Aunt Sophie, Aunt Mavis, we came to tell you something!"

"You're going to sue us!" Sophie exclaimed. Handkerchiefs covered both faces as the ladies started to cry again.

"Hilary—" Brink growled.

"Aunt Sophie, look here!" Hilary shouted, jumping to her feet. She waved her diamond-studded hand at them.

Sophie gasped. "Mavis, look! Why, I believe these young people are engaged. He's going to be our relative! Saville will be back in the family again!"

Eleven

In the car Brink repeated grimly, "This doesn't mean that the aunts will get the house. And don't try to do me in so you'll inherit and they'll get it."

"Do you in? What a thought. How about by exhaustion?" Hilary drawled in a throaty voice, running her hand along his thigh. "That might be an interesting goal."

He grinned. "When you put it that way, I can't wait!"

She snuggled next to him. "Let's change the subject from my aunts."

"I thought we already had," he exclaimed, hugging her. And the house, the aunts, and the distant future weren't brought up again that night.

Brink rented a yacht, and they spent the following night on the river, making love in the moonlight. Brink assured her there was no one within miles to see them. She was delighted to discover he was staying until Monday to investigate a local landfill company that was going up for sale.

On Monday afternoon, as Hilary worked in the shop, she heard the brass bell jingle. She looked up in time to see Brink sweep through the door.

"Hi," he said. "Are you here alone?"

"Yes, you lucky man! Come back to my office and let me show you my etchings, darling!" she teased.

"Best offer I've had today! Just a minute." He slipped the bolt on the front door and turned the sign to read, "Closed."

"You'll ruin my reputation—and my business! I never close early," she said with a smile.

"You did today."

In her office, Hilary rushed into his arms and clung to him. He raised his head. "Any employees coming back this afternoon?"

"No," she whispered, pulling his head back down.

Reaching behind her, he lowered the zipper of her blue cotton dress and pushed it gently off her shoulders. Then he stepped back to slip off his suit coat.

Her breasts tingled as his gaze lingered. She waited, watching him while he undressed. As he unfastened his belt and pulled off his shirt and tie, his gaze seared her skin, like warm fingers over her flesh. She wore only scanty pink lace underwear, a white garter belt, and stockings. He trailed his fingers along a bare spot on the inside of her thigh, just above her stockings, and she gasped. "You're beautiful," he whispered. "Take those things off."

She did, licking her lips as she unfastened her bra and let it fall. He sucked in his breath, making his broad chest expand. Then he reached out to cup her breasts in his callused hands, bending his head.

She threw back her head and closed her eyes, yielding to desire while he pulled her down on the love seat and moved between her legs.

"I can't wait," he whispered.

Later, as she was dressing, she smiled at him. "My office will never seem quite the same."

"I hope not. I don't want you to forget me. At work or at home."

"I couldn't forget you!"

He sighed. "I want to look at the collection in your shop. I've never had the chance."

"You had a chance. You were just too busy trying to run Scott away—and you succeeded."

"You didn't seem to mind."

"I sure didn't. Come on. I'll show you around."

Within minutes she realized he was quite an expert as he ran his finger along the back of a chair. "Nice. Aubusson tapestry. A Régence *fauteuil*, early 1700s."

"If you ever want a job, I'll hire you," she said, delighted that he really did know his antiques.

He grinned at her and touched the tip of her nose with a flick of his forefinger, winking at her. "Don't sound so damn surprised! There you go again, jumping to hasty conclusions, just like you did the day I met you."

"How can someone who works in landfill know and love antiques! I don't understand you!"

"And I, sweetie, don't understand how someone with marvelous talent can pitch it aside and do something totally removed from it," he said pleasantly.

"That's entirely different," she said, wondering if she thought he was more handsome with his hair neatly combed or slightly tousled, as it was now. She wanted to reach up and run her fingers through it, but they were in the shop; anyone walking past could see them through the wide glass windows. He proceded down the aisle, and she followed, still amazed at him.

"I'll be damned! An ambry! Where did you get this?" he asked, admiring a carved cabinet.

"I found it here in Mississippi, at an estate sale. It's oak, from a church in England, late fifteenth century."

"Ah, Hilary! Ah, Lordy!" He shook his head in wonder, then pointed to another piece. "I didn't see this before. It's Chippendale."

"It dates from 1775," she said. "We haven't had it long. I acquired it just before my trip to Los Angeles."

"How much is it?" he asked, then found the tag. "This would be perfect in our den."

"Brink, we don't have a den."

"We will."

"You're serious!"

"Of course I am. It's magnificent! Mark this sold," he said, pulling out a checkbook.

"Put away your checkbook! Good grief! Since we're going to be the same family, it's yours now too."

"There goes your shrewd business sense right out the window. We're not family yet, and I'll pay for what I want, just the same as any other customer. It keeps the books straight. I'll expect you to pay me if you use my landfill services."

"Sure, sure!"

"Mark it sold, Hilary." Suddenly he frowned. "Lord, I'm sorry. It's going to be your house. Do you want this clock?"

"Sure. You can fill the house with antiques! I don't care as long as you're in bed with me at night."

His frown vanished. "What a woman! And what an antique dealer. These are really gems!"

"But they're just antiques, Brink. You seem to love them more than me. You really do like *things* an awful lot."

He looked startled, then he caught her arms and pulled her hard against his chest.

"Hey, what—"

His mouth came down on hers, opening it to kiss her wildly. He persisted, despite her gentle struggle, until finally she wound her arms around him and returned his kisses. When he slipped his hand to the neck of her dress, her wits returned.

"Brink! You'll embarrass me to pieces! Anyone can see us!" She looked around frantically.

"I want you to know that I'm more taken with a flesh-and-blood woman than with any *thing* in this store. And I'm going to prove it to you."

"I believe you!" she said breathlessly, stepping back out of his reach.

There was a twinkle in his eye as he winked.

"You are so unpredictable!" she said.

"Me?" he said with feigned innocence. He continued browsing, pausing to look in a glass case at a pair of dueling pistols. "Interesting." He moved on and stopped. "A Tiffany lamp, isn't it?"

"Yes, glass and bronze."

"Do you like it?"

"Of course, or I wouldn't have bought it."

"It would look good in the same room with the grandfather clock, don't you think?"

When she laughed, he turned around to look at her quizzically. "What's so funny?"

"Don't *I* think! Admit it. You desperately want that lamp!"

"I won't buy it if you don't want it. Tell you what. I'll have these things shipped to California, and you can decorate the house we build here any way you want."

"That's a deal."

He wandered down an aisle toward the back while she straightened some china figurines.

"Hilary!"

"Don't tell me," she said, going to see what he had found. "Mark it sold."

"If you like it."

"It's a good thing you're marrying into the business, or you'd go broke. I never heard of an antique-aholic until now."

"This armoire is a rare piece. Do you like it?"

"Yes. Mark it sold?"

He smiled. "Right."

"The landfill business must be doing well," she said.

"It is. And I've had some lucky investments." He winked at her. "You could just retire and paint, you know. You wouldn't have to change your life-style. And Los Angeles would be a marvelous place to start your career."

"I'll keep that in the back if my mind," she said, shocked to realize his business might be worth a fortune. His casual selection of the highest-priced antiques in the store made her realize there was a lot about Brink she didn't know.

And no matter how much he argued the point, he did have a materialistic streak. It disturbed her, because she loved people so much. Sophie and Mavis were far more important than Saville. And she knew she would feel the same way, even if she wasn't a blood relative of theirs.

He held up a crystal decanter. "This is nice." He glanced at her, then set the decanter down carefully.

"What's wrong?" he asked, placing his hands on her shoulders.

"I'm still afraid that you don't realize how important people are."

"Sure I do. And to prove it, I'll take one special person to dinner. We need to celebrate the new business we are going to own in Natchez."

"Brink! You found a business in one day?"

"Call it the luck of the Claiborns! Yeah. It wasn't going to be for sale for another month. The owner, a man named Sidney Thorpe, wants to retire. The company is a little smaller than I wanted, but there's room for expansion. I feel lucky to have found it. Shall we go celebrate?"

"Brink," she said, looking past him at the long pink Cadillac at the curb.

"Oh, Lord, it's Mavis!" He caught her arm and ducked, pulling her down beside him. "We're not spending the evening with your aunts!"

"Brink, let me up! She'll be scandalized if she sees us down here on the floor."

"Hilary, I can't deal with them tonight."

The doorknob rattled, then Mavis tapped on the glass, her voice faintly wafting through the shop. "Yoo hoo! Hilary! Hilary!"

"I have to answer. She'll go around in back and see my car. Where's your car?"

"On the side. She can't see you if you don't stand up. Crawl down the aisle and let's get out of here."

"Brink!"

He leaned forward and kissed her fully on the mouth, then pulled back. "Crawl, honey!"

She squatted down and walked, suddenly laughing. "Brink, this is absurd!"

"My nervous system doesn't think so! If I have to eat turnip greens tonight, *I'll* need tranquilizers. And it isn't a damn bit funny!"

Hilary glanced over her shoulder and laughed, watching him follow in a far more coordinated duck walk. In the hall they stood up, and Hilary grabbed her purse from the office.

"Hurry, dammit!"

"If she comes around the building while we're here, we'll wait. I wouldn't want to deliberately hurt her feelings."

"It's a deal. Come on," he said, taking her keys and her arm as they rushed outside and slid into her car.

"This is really terrible, Brink."

"What was it when they tried to knock me out?"

"I'll admit, that was bad too."

He paused at the entrance to the street.

"She isn't in sight. Go ahead." She watched until they turned the corner. "Brink, you're going to marry me. I can't avoid my aunts forever."

He took a deep breath. "I know. I'll manage to deal with them when I have to, but tonight is special. I want to celebrate the new business." He glanced at her and reached over to take her hand. "And I have to go back to Los Angeles tomorrow afternoon, after we sign the contracts. I want you all to myself tonight."

She squeezed his hand. "That sounds just fine with me."

Later, over broiled lobster at The Briars, beside a wide window, Brink studied Hilary.

"A penny for your thoughts," she said softly.

"I'm impressed."

"By what?"

"You. Your shop. You have marvelous things."

"Thank you," she said, feeling warmed by his praise. "Maybe you should go into business with me."

"I'd like to, but the landfill business is too damn good right now to quit."

"Are you a workaholic?"

"Do I act like one?"

She smiled at him as his calf brushed against hers. "No, you don't."

"Come home with me, Hilary, and let me show you Los Angeles."

It was on the tip of her tongue to refuse politely, to tell him all the practical reasons she couldn't, but as she gazed into his compelling blue eyes and saw the love that showed so plainly, she nodded. "I'll see what I can work out at the store."

He smiled at her, and she wanted to melt into his arms. She craved his touch, yearned to feel his warm lips upon hers. The lobster was no longer appealing. She sat quietly until Brink put down his fork.

"You're not eating."

She shrugged. "That isn't what I want right now."

He turned his head to signal to the waiter. In minutes they were in the car headed to her place.

When they stepped inside the back door, he lifted her into his arms and carried her into the darkened bedroom. One small light burned in the adjoining bath, but the moon was bright, illuminating the room with its silvery sheen.

Brink set her on her feet. "Now I can do all the

things I've been wanting to do for hours," he said, nibbling her ear and trailing kisses to her mouth. "How long since I last told you I love you?"

"Eight minutes and forty-six seconds," she murmured happily.

"Little liar!" he accused. Then his mouth covered hers and she was lost. She slid her hands over his arms, feeling the powerful muscles as he crushed her to him, his arousal pressing against her. She groaned, wanting to feel his bare skin, wanting to hold him, to kiss him, to touch him.

"I love you, Brink," she whispered, desire flaming through her like a raging bonfire.

She flew home with him the next afternoon and spent a glorious week in Los Angeles. He bought her a gorgeous black dress on Rodeo Drive, took her to Universal Studios and the Los Angeles Music Center, and treated her to scrumptious meals. But most of their time was spent at home in his big bed. Once, she rolled over and frowned at him. "Brink, you'll be tired of me by the time we get married and have a honeymoon."

He gave her a fatuous smile and reached out lazily to tug the sheet out of her hands, revealing her bare breasts. His forefinger made a slow trail back and forth across her skin, slipping lower and lower from her collarbone, down between her breasts to her waist.

"You think so?" he asked in a husky voice, his blue eyes filled with smoldering desire.

His finger traced a circle around her nipple, and he watched as she became swiftly aroused. He wanted her constantly. He couldn't concentrate at work; images of her in his arms, in bed with him, came to mind all during the day. On the days he had to work, he couldn't wait to get home at night to be with her.

With satisfaction and excitement, he watched her eyes darken. Hilary caught his hand to kiss his fingers, then purposefully placed it back on her breast. Her head lolled back and she closed her eyes momentarily, only to open them in seconds. She looked at him intently, her gaze drifting down the length of him as her fingers moved over his thigh to caress him. With a groan he covered her, crushing her in his arms.

Brink flew back to Natchez with her and was able to stay the following weekend. On Friday night they dined with Sophie and Mavis, but Brink insisted on taking them all out to eat. Afterward they sat at the aunts' house, where Sophie dug out old, tattered scrapbooks and showed Brink their childhood pictures taken at Saville. To Hilary's amazement, he lost the careful courtesy he always accorded the aunts and became totally engrossed in the pictures, lingering over them until Sophie's head was nodding and Mavis was stifling yawns. Hilary finally took the scrapbooks from him, and they said good night. In the car she turned to him. "I'm proud of you. You were very nice to them tonight."

"To tell the truth, I had a good time." He grinned. "See what you've done to me? I'm beginning to like them."

"Good!" she said, enormously pleased.

"And what I like most of all about them," he said as they parked in front of her house, "is their niece." He leaned across the car to kiss her. After a moment he said, "Let's go inside."

"I thought you'd never ask."

During the next two weeks Brink flew back and forth between Los Angeles and Natchez, dividing his time between the two places.

June was nearly over. Hilary spent the third week of June in bliss, looking at wedding magazines, planning for the future, talking on the phone to Brink, relishing every moment with him. At night in her room she lay in bed, on fire with longing, wondering how they would work out living in both Natchez and Los Angeles. They couldn't go back and forth constantly, as he was doing now. There were so many things to discuss, but every time they were alone together, instead of making plans, they ended up making love.

She hired a cleaning woman to go once a week to the Wakefield house, and Brink hired the woman to go twice a week to Saville. Next she hired painters to repaint the outside of the house, something her aunts thought totally unnecessary, so Hilary paid for it out of her savings.

On Friday she received a phone call at nine in the morning. The moment she heard Brink's voice, she knew something was wrong.

"Hon, I wanted to let you know. I'm flying in earlier than I'd planned. They called me from the nursing home. Grandpa passed away in his sleep, about thirty minutes ago."

"Brink, I'm so sorry."

"I knew this was coming. I'm glad I was able to see more of him these last few weeks. At least it was peaceful for him. He had a long, good life. You know, he would have been ninety-three this year. . . . Anyway, I'll call you as soon as I get into town. See you soon, honey. I love you."

She replaced the receiver and phoned her aunts to break the news, then she went home to be ready when Brink arrived.

When Hilary opened the door, he crushed her in his arms. To her relief he seemed composed; he had accepted his grandfather's death with grace and dignity.

The funeral was the next morning. The weekend and the next week passed in a haze while Brink was busy taking care of so many details.

The following Sunday afternoon, after Brink had flown back to Los Angeles, Hilary was paying bills at her kitchen table when the phone rang. She answered to hear Sophie crying softly.

"Hilary. He's done it! He's finally done it!"

Twelve

"Who's done what?" Hilary asked, turning a page in her checkbook.

"Your fiancé!" Sophie exclaimed.

Hilary blinked, forgetting the bills in front of her. "Brink?" She began to get a premonition of disaster as an image of Saville flashed into mind.

"We had Sam Jarvis call him about buying Saville. We didn't want to up and call with his poor grandfather barely laid to rest, so we waited. It was only decent and right to wait."

"Of course. What's happened, Aunt Sophie?"

"Yesterday he said he wouldn't put it on the market. Today, when Sam called him, he said he's showing it to a group of buyers from Jackson. They're going to make our home into a museum!" She began to sob.

Hilary felt as if she had received an electric shock. She sat up straighter, staring into space with a frown. He had actually done it. He was marrying into the family, yet he had turned right around and broken her aunts' hearts. To make matters worse, he had been in Natchez all week and hadn't said one word to her about it. Not one word! Her temper began to soar.

"Has he signed any papers?"

"I don't think so. Hilary, it's our home. Mavis and I wanted so badly to go back to Saville. Why won't he listen?"

"He'll listen. I'll call you back. In the meantime, stop worrying," she said, becoming angrier by the minute.

She punched the numbers to call him, listened to the rings, and heard his deep voice say hello.

"You snake in the grass!" she snapped, her temper flaring.

"Hey! Hilary? What on earth?"

"Saville."

"Oh. Now, listen. I never said I was going to let your aunts have the house. Just because . . ."

"Just because we're getting married doesn't mean you have to love them, but it does mean you have to be decent to them. They're willing to pay any price. And you misled me! You know I thought you were softening. You're ready to close a deal, aren't you?"

"I think I better catch a flight right back to Natchez. I'll be there on the next plane."

"Brink Claiborn—" The phone clicked in her ear, and she stared at it. "Dammit!" She slammed down the receiver, picked up the phone directory, and called to find out when the next flight would arrive from Los Angeles via commuter to Alexandria.

She found he couldn't make connections and arrive in Alexandria until eight in the morning. When he did, she would be waiting.

By the next morning, her temper hadn't cooled one whit. She waited outside in the warm summer air that promised the day would be a muggy scorcher before it was over. That morning she had spent an hour bathing, fixing her hair, and dressing in her most sophisticated tailored dress, because she wanted to look her best that evening. Her hair was fastened in a smooth chignon behind her head, the shorter hair around her face feathered away from her forehead. She wore silver hoop earrings and a straight black sleeveless cotton dress with a straight skirt that was slit to the knee in front. She had chosen to wear her highest black heels—all the better to look him straight in the eye.

Hilary watched the plane land on the airport's only runway. The attendants wheeled the ladder up to the door and then the passengers disembarked. She spotted Brink, striding toward her. He wore a casual blue shirt, open at the throat, and tan slacks; his hair was neatly combed, the unruly curls under control. His gaze swept over the crowd, met hers, and stayed fixed as he threaded his way around people to reach her.

Only his eyes revealed his anger. She saw the flash of fire in them and suspected her own fury could match his. Without a word he took her arm and led her through the gate to her car. He opened the door for her, but before she could sit down, he caught her arm, turning her to face him.

"When you took my ring and accepted, I said I couldn't change my ways. You said you'd take me just as I was. And you knew then exactly what I intended for Saville."

"I hoped you would soften up and change your

mind. I'm not breaking our engagement, unless you want your ring back," she said evenly.

"No, I don't." His blue eyes were fierce, but steady. An electric current ignited between them in spite of their differences, in spite of their anger. Suddenly he framed her face with his hands. His gaze lowered to her mouth, and he leaned forward to kiss her.

She didn't want him to kiss her; she wanted to talk. She tried to twist her head away, but his hands held her tightly. His mouth covered her protest, kissing her passionately. Crushing her in his arms, he backed her against the car, pressing against her, kissing her wildly until he began to get the response he wanted.

Brink was in a rage, trying to control his temper, yet at the same time wanting her more than ever. She had taken his breath away when he'd first spotted her, looking cool and remote. Only now, her green eyes revealed the fiery storm in her heart. And all he wanted to do was take her home and peel away the black dress and make love to her until all this nonsense was forgotten. But every time he thought about how angry she was, he became angry in return, because he had never promised to change. Not once; not at any time.

He kissed her, unleashing his anger and passion, crushing her desirable softness to him, wanting to demolish her self-control and fury.

Finally he felt her respond. Her body softened, fitting against his, and her arm slipped around his neck. And then she kissed him in return.

When he raised his head abruptly, her lips were parted, her eyes closed, her breasts pressed against his chest.

"Get in and we'll talk at your house," he demanded.

Finally they were in her living room, facing each other. She moved away from him to the other side of the coffee table. He jammed his hands in his pockets, turning to her.

"I just don't understand how you can do this to them."

"You've known what I wanted for Saville from day one, so this shouldn't be any surprise. My actions aren't any different than my intentions last week, or the week before that, or the week before that."

"I don't think I ever really believed you could be so hard-hearted!"

"Dammit, that isn't being hard-hearted! It's preserving what I love."

"All you think about is that house."

"Look, Hilary, I haven't tried to make your life over—even though there's room for you to make some changes!"

"Don't try to change the subject! And what are you talking about? *What* could I change in my life?"

"Not letting all your talent go to waste!"

"Oh, that!"

"Yes, that! It's absurd for you to be afraid to compete. I offered to foot the bills while you painted. You need to overcome your fears. But I haven't tried to make you over or change you, have I?"

· "Not until now."

"And I'm not now. I'm merely pointing out that I think you're wrong, but it's your business."

"And I suppose Saville is yours."

"Damn right it is!"

"And if this had happened in September or October, after we had said our vows, would it still be only your business?"

He frowned. "I intended to take care of it before the wedding," he said quietly, "because I didn't want it to become an issue later."

"That's cruel! You've toured the house with my aunts, fascinated when they told us about their childhood! You've lingered over their old photographs and mementos. They may not have many years left. Yet instead of making their golden years supremely happy, you're ruining them!"

"Aw, come on! I grew up in Saville too. I want to preserve the home I love and share it with others. They can take the tour anytime they want. They can volunteer to show it."

"That isn't the same!"

"I can't bear to see it go to ruin."

"You could keep it and let them rent it, and we could handle the maintenance. I would pay for it myself, Brink. You wouldn't have to spend a dime of your money!"

"Hilary, you're pushing," he said, clenching his fists.

"All you're interested in is things. Just things! I can't imagine how you ever got worked up enough to propose to me."

"I did it because I fell in love with you, something I definitely didn't plan!"

"And what does that mean?"

He crossed the room in angry strides, ignoring her protests, yanking her into his arms. Tears swam in her wide green eyes, until he kissed them away. She looked gorgeous; he would never forget that first glimpse of her in the sexy black dress. How she had aroused him and sent desire coursing through his veins! His fingers yanked at the buttons and slipped beneath the cotton.

She caught his wrist and tried to pull his hand away, but he tightened his grip and kissed her deeply. His fingers found her nipple and caressed her until he felt her yield. When he had shoved away her clothing, she clung to him wildly, her hips thrusting against him. His fingers tugged through her hair, sending pins flying. Finally, soft, silken strands tumbled over his hands.

He pushed her down on the sofa, shifting and twisting to get his clothes off without breaking away from her. Then he stood over her, looking down. She lay with her hair swirling behind her head, some golden locks curling on her bare shoulders. Her breasts were thrust toward him, tantalizing him. She was ivory and dusky pink and gold. Her green eyes were as stormy as ever, but they were filled with desire too.

"I love you," he said huskily.

"I love you too," she said, reaching for him. He slid between her legs, taking her swiftly, watching her and waiting until she cried out in ecstasy. His voice mingled with hers and release surged through him, making him shudder with each thrust.

He held her, relishing her softness beneath him. Minutes later he realized that she was crying softly. "Hilary?"

"I don't want to fight you. And I can't bear what's happening."

"Shh . . . don't cry. Hold me. You looked so damn beautiful tonight, Hilary." He kissed her cheek. They hadn't solved anything, but he hadn't been able to stop himself from reaching for her.

Without much conversation they showered and dressed. Hilary pulled on her white cotton night-gown and blue robe. In the kitchen, facing him from across the table, she thought how handsome he was. His hair was a tangle of curls, his shirt was loose and open, and it required great restraint not to reach across and stroke his muscular chest.

Only his stormy blue eyes held her back.

Hilary sat toying with her wineglass. There was very little to say.

"There isn't any way I can get you to reconsider?" she asked quietly.

"Nothing's changed. I've never at any time prom-ised to hand over Saville, to sell them Saville, to rent it to them. And I haven't given the slightest indica-tion of changing my mind."

"That doesn't mean you can't change it now. You're making such a colossal mistake. It's so cold and unfeeling."

"Aw, hell. I've had plans for that place since I learned I was going to inherit it."

"What time do you leave tomorrow to go back to California?"

"Not until four o'clock."

"Tomorrow, go with me to see Mavis and Sophie."

He groaned. "I don't want them crying all over me."

"I have a key to the house. We can go while they're at church. I don't think you've looked at their house lately."

"I know. You hired a maid and you've had the house painted. But, honey, I want a museum that thousands of people can enjoy. Instead of two ladies loving it, many, many people can enjoy it and learn about our heritage."

She sat back, staring at him. They were at logger-heads, and she couldn't see any solution. The silence was thick; the world outside quiet. Rubbing the bridge of her nose to fight back tears, she looked beyond him. "Maybe what's between us is purely physical," she said carefully.

"I don't think so, Hilary," he replied solemnly, "or I wouldn't have asked you to marry me. I would have just tried to seduce you."

She stared down at the floor.

"Honey," he said, studying the glossy sheen to her hair. She shook back her hair and looked at him. Her eyes were glassy with tears.

"Come here," he said gently, pushing back his chair.

Without a flicker of expression she went to him. He pulled her down carefully, to sit on his lap. "It's three in the morning. Think we could put our problems aside, keep the love we have, and go get some sleep?"

She nodded. "I'll try."

He turned out the light as they left the kitchen. Minutes later, in bed, he pulled her close in his arms and kissed her cheek.

Suddenly she turned to hug him, and he felt a knot form in his throat. He squeezed her tightly against his chest and kissed her again. In moments he was breathing deeply and evenly, fast asleep.

Hilary lay awake with her head on his chest, wondering why he was so stubborn. And she worried about the future. Twice that night she had been on the verge of giving him back his ring. And she had realized that in many ways she still didn't know Brink very well. They had a lot in common—they had talked about religion, philosophy, grocery buying, families, all sorts of things—yet how well did she really know him?

She ran her fingers lightly across his chest, studying his virile body. He looked powerful even when he was asleep. She fought the urge to lean down and kiss him. How she loved him! But Hilary was caught in a terrible dilemma. If he broke her aunts' hearts, Hilary didn't know how she and Brink could build a solid relationship. And if Brink remained attached to material things, was he really the man she wanted to share her life with?

He was so stubborn!

She pulled off the ring, looked at him, letting her gaze drift down his naked length. Tears rolled down her cheeks. She couldn't do it. She cried silently as she slipped the ring back on her finger, trying to ignore the terrible premonition that they might not be able to iron out their differences.

At breakfast they ate only thin slices of toast and coffee. Their conversation was brief, dwindling into silence.

Brink sat across from her, his long legs stretched out, his hands jammed into his pockets. In spite of their problems, he felt a faint twinge of amusement and admiration.

She might not like competition, might not think she was aggressive enough to fight for a career, but he knew better. She was fighting him with as much cool tact as some of the best businessmen he had encountered. He knew she had dressed in her best to meet him the night before. She had dressed accordingly that morning. No rumpled old robe and gown.

When he had come to the kitchen, he had found her with her hair fastened in a chignon, her makeup enhancing her natural loveliness, stockings on her legs, pale blue low-heeled pumps that matched her tailored cotton dress. She was ready to match wits and she obviously wanted every advantage possible.

She had wrecked his peaceful life. He wasn't going to let her destroy all his future plans over two little old ladies who would be lost in a big house like Saville.

He pushed out a chair with his toe. "Come sit down and let's talk a little more about this. Silence isn't going to solve anything. If we want a solution, we're going to have to have a discussion."

"Of course. You look amused."

He shrugged. "You know, you're holding your own quite well with me now."

"The outcome remains to be seen."

"Yeah. Tell me something, what would Mavis and Sophie do all the time in that big house?"

A flicker of surprise came to her eyes, and Brink felt a degree of satisfaction. "I don't think any of you, not Mavis or Sophie or you, have really stopped to think what their lives would be like. I'll bet they simply want to go back to relive old memories. When they lived there, their parents were there. The household had servants—it was a home filled with people. All those rooms and just two little old ladies? And Mavis hobbles around now because of her arthritis."

"There are two downstairs bedrooms, as you know."

"And they would probably live down there and let the upper floor go to ruin."

"Brink, I'll keep the upper floor from going to ruin!"

"You haven't listened to me or given one second's thought to what I was saying."

"Brink, forget the damn museum! And no matter how much I love you, I'll never understand this—this selfish materialism!"

Her words stung and made him angry. "That's damn foolishness!"

"As far as I'm concerned, there is not one antique in my shop as important as any one person in this town! Any person! Can you say the same?"

"No, I can't. I can't even believe you really feel that way."

They glared at each other in silence. He pushed away his chair and stood up. She came to her feet and faced him.

"How are we going to work this out between us? I need to go back to Los Angeles today."

"Then you'd better go," she said, and he saw the bright glimmer of tears in her eyes. He hurt badly, but he couldn't agree with her. She was soft and impractical.

"I can see right now, Brink, that Saville is more important to you than what we have between us."

"That's not a damn bit so!" he snapped. "What you're saying is do this your way or I'm callous and cold and don't love you!"

"No, I didn't say that."

"Hilary, would you be a little more realistic and practical?" he asked in a strained voice, trying to curb his impatience. "You don't think I listen to you. I don't think you're listening to me or giving one second's consideration to anything I've said."

"Of course I have! And I always come right back to the same conclusion."

As he watched her, tears filled her eyes, threatening to spill over. Transfixed, he stared as she lifted her hands and pulled off her ring.

Pain filled him. He wanted to shove the ring back on her hands, crush her in his arms, kiss away their differences as he had the night before, but he knew it wouldn't accomplish a thing. It would only prolong the inevitable.

"I can't keep this, Brink. There are just too many problems between us."

"Do they know they're causing you to break your engagement?"

"Of course not! And don't you—"

"Oh, hell! I wouldn't go tell them. You must think I don't have any heart at all," he said quietly. He had to leave before he lost his cool control. With a burning knot in his throat, pain and anger raging inside him, he took the ring.

"Dammit!" he snapped, suddenly turning back to her, unable to control himself as he yanked her into his arms and kissed her hard.

Finally he could release her. Blindly he stormed out of the house without a good-bye. He slammed into his car, oblivious of the squeal of tires when he pulled away from the curb. He drove straight to Saville and skidded to a halt in the driveway, sending gravel and dust flying behind the car. Frozen in the driver's seat, he stared at the old house.

At home, Hilary remained in the same spot long after the roar of the car outside had faded into silence. She rubbed her bare finger, unaware of her hot tears. She wanted Brink so badly. He had so many wonderful qualities, but she couldn't live with his obsession for material things.

She moved woodenly through the house to close and lock the door, staring outside. Everywhere she looked, she saw Brink—lounging on the patio, moving through the kitchen, lying across her bed. . . .

The day was the longest and the most painful in her life. All Brink's good points became magnified, yet it was impossible to overcome this one problem. She went over and over their arguments and knew that even if she capitulated, he was probably through with her forever.

She made arrangements for someone to fill in for her at the store, because she couldn't bear to go to work. She told her assistant to tell people she was out of town, but actually, if they needed her, she would be at home.

"Anything I can help with?" Becky asked.

"No, but thanks. I need some time to myself. I gave Brink back his ring."

"Oh! I'm sorry."

"Thanks, Becky. I don't want Mavis and Sophie to know yet."

"Sure, I won't say a word. I hope you work it out."

"Thanks."

Work it out? It was over. Finished. Hilary put her head in her hands and cried.

During the quiet of the next two days she had nothing to do, nothing she could concentrate on. In a daze of pain and hurt and sorrow, she moved through the house, doing only what she had to do. Her appetite was gone, and sleep was impossible.

Every time she passed the seascape of Brink's beach, the painting conjured up painful memories. One afternoon she decided to put her paintings away until life improved.

Carefully she began to stack them in the utility-room closet. Now and then she paused to study them, thinking how a touch here or there might have been better, deciding that some were finished and just fine the way they were.

And as she shifted them from room to room she remembered all of Brink's arguments about her talent. She was focusing on one drawing as a frightening revelation came to her.

She had accused Brink of having a closed mind and not listening or considering her arguments, but had she done the same with him?

He hadn't persisted about her talent, although he had been firm in his opinions. She sat down and stared at a painting she had done of a shop on Silver Street, a bluff in the background. And she realized she hadn't listened to him. Long ago she had made up her mind she wouldn't pursue art, and she hadn't once reconsidered. Maybe she had been just as stubborn and close-minded about Saville. Shocked, she stared into space, losing all track of time as she rethought everything from Brink's standpoint. Mavis and Sophie might be lost in the big house, as he'd said. And they might miss their lovely little house, especially Mavis, who had lived there since she'd first married Tom.

Hilary trembled as she realized she had done just exactly what she had accused Brink of doing. She'd been as stubborn as a mule!

As she began to rethink the arguments, another

thought loomed much larger. She would rather try to solve problems with Brink than without him. Her hands shook as she dialed his office, only to be told that he had left town.

She drew a deep breath, trying to dispel the pain. She felt a desperate need to find him. Her fingers still shook with urgency as she dialed and made arrangements for the next flight she could catch to Los Angeles.

And then she dashed to her room to dress, pausing only a moment to call Becky and tell her where she was going.

"I'm glad!" Becky said with eagerness.

"Not half as much as I am," Hilary said, feeling as if the weight of the world had been lifted off her heart.

She wore a tailored navy skirt and a pale blue blouse, leaving her hair to fall free. And then she was gone.

The long trip gave her plenty of time to think and plan. When she stepped off the plane at LAX, she had to fight the urge for a cab. She went straight to a motel, registered, and then began the long wait, trying to call Brink's house, trying again at his office. On the second call to his house, the receiver lifted and a woman answered. Hilary's breathing stopped dead.

Thirteen

"Is Brink there?" Hilary asked.

"No, I'm sorry, he's out of town. Can I take a message?"

Hilary hurt all over. Mortified, she wanted to hang up. Instead, she asked, "Do you know when he'll be back?"

"No. He didn't give a definite time. He's in Mississippi. If you'll leave your number—"

"Who is this?" Hilary asked.

"I'm his next-door neighbor—"

"Kiki! This is Hilary."

"Oh? I thought—he's in Mississippi. I'm just here to take in his paper and mail. We trade off. Say, congratulations! And I think I can add an I-told-you-so."

He hadn't told Kiki about the broken engagement! Hilary wanted to jump in the air for joy.

"Thanks, Kiki. I'll call him. I know where to find him."

Immediately she dialed the antique shop.

Before Becky could finish saying hello, Hilary interrupted her.

"Becky, it's me, Hilary. Listen, I expect—"

"Hilary! Guess who was just here about an hour after you left home?" The laughter in her voice was evident.

"I know. Brink."

"Where are you now?"

"I'm in California."

"He said to tell you not to go away."

"I wouldn't dream of it!" she answered happily.

"I'm so glad."

"I am too. See you soon."

"Maybe. Bye."

Hilary replaced the receiver, looked down at her tailored navy skirt and blue blouse, and wished she had taken more time and worn something very special.

On impulse she decided to go shopping while she waited for Brink, because this was a very special day. She called a cab and stepped out into the hot sunshine, heading toward the motel lobby.

The glass doors at a side entrance swung open, and a tall man emerged. Hilary stopped, her heart and lungs ceasing to function for seconds as she stared at Brink coming toward her.

He was more handsome than ever! She ran, throwing herself into his arms. He caught her, crushing the breath from her lungs.

"Hey!" He kissed her hungrily, passionately, pausing only for a second to whisper, "Where's the key to your room?"

She reached into her pocket and handed it to

him. He scooped her into his arms, opened the door, then kicked it shut when they were inside.

He set her on her feet, reached into his pocket, and withdrew the ring to slip it back on her finger. "This goes on . . ."

The blatant desire in his expression made her inhale deeply and reach for him.

". . . and this comes off," he whispered huskily, his hand going to the top button of her blouse.

"How did you get back here so fast?" she asked softly.

"Charter." Brink watched her as he unbuttoned her blouse. His heart pounded with longing. He wanted to love her until she fainted. And he saw the desire plainly evident in her eyes. He pushed away her blouse, and his eyebrows arched as he cupped her lovely, full breasts.

"I dressed in a hurry."

"We'll get back to the reasons for that later," he said huskily, bending his head to touch the tip of her nipple with his tongue. She gasped, winding her fingers in his hair for a moment, then trailing them down over his throat to tug at his shirt.

An hour later she lay in his arms in bed, the dusky light of late afternoon fading as she trailed her fingers through the thick mat of hair on his chest.

"Want to talk now?" she whispered.

"For about ten minutes," he answered, smiling at her, letting his fingers drift back and forth lazily on her bare hip.

"You were right," they both said in unison, and laughed.

He pulled her on top of him and smiled at her. "I hope you learned something from this."

"I did. And I hope you did too."

"I'll tell you what I learned. Life isn't worth a damn without you. And Saville can fall into the Mississippi for all I care, if it means losing you."

"Brink!"

He frowned. "Don't sound so damn surprised. Why did you think I flew to Mississippi? Why did you come out here?"

"To tell you I hadn't really listened with an open mind. I might try letting you support me in L.A. while I paint. . . ."

"Ah, that's my girl. I knew I was making a wise choice."

"Talk about a fatuous male!"

He chuckled. "And Mavis and Sophie can have a lifetime estate in Saville. When we get time after the honeymoon, I'll have the papers drawn up."

"Sweetie!" she squealed, hugging him and sitting up. "Let me show you my gratitude, darling," she said in a teasing, exaggerated drawl. She leaned down to trail her tongue over his flat stomach.

He moaned and rolled her over. All amusement was gone from his face as he lay on top of her. "People are more important, and if I ever slip back into my old ways, just remind me. I don't ever want to be without you again."

"Oh, Brink!" She gasped, seeing the love in his blue eyes.

He crushed her in his arms, and Hilary sighed with contentment. "Thank heaven for dynamite!"

Brink chuckled softly. "What good has dynamite done you?"

"If that had been just plain old ground, you might not have paid any attention to me."

"I would have paid attention, but I wouldn't have had to react so violently. I guess you're right again. Thank heaven for dynamite!"

He kissed her, and she clung to him, blissfully looking forward to their future.

THE EDITOR'S CORNER

We are preparing to light five huge candles on our LOVESWEPT birthday cake next month. And, because we are celebrating this special anniversary, I've asked to take back the writing of the "Editor's Corner" to make a lot of special announcements.

You have a gala month to look forward to with wonderful books both in the LOVESWEPT line and in the Bantam Books general list. The historical Delaney trilogy is coming and will go on sale at the same time the LOVESWEPTs do. Here's what you have to anticipate.

THE DELANEYS, THE UNTAMED YEARS

Historical splendor of post-Civil War America.
Unforgettable characters who founded the Delaney Dynasty
Spellbinding adventure ablaze with passion.

COPPER FIRE
By Fayrene Preston
Set in the Colorado Territory, 1873, **COPPER FIRE** tells the story of the tenderhearted spitfire Brianne Delaney, whose search for her kidnapped twin brother leads her into the arms of a rugged, ruthless man.

WILD SILVER
By Iris Johansen
From Imperial Russia to the Mississippi delta, 1874, **WILD SILVER** follows the exquisite half-Apache outcast, Silver Delaney, who is held captive on a riverboat by its mysterious owner, a young and irresistible, fallen Russian prince.

GOLDEN FLAMES
By Kay Hooper
Moving from New York to the New Mexico/Arizona border, 1870, **GOLDEN FLAMES** trails Falcon Delaney, the broodingly handsome loner who's spent years tracing a stolen cache of Union gold. But now he turns his skills to tracking the secrets of the bewitching woman who has stolen his soul.

And, going on sale April 20, 1988, as part of Bantam's Grand Slam promotion you will see copies everywhere of the breathtaking and spine-tingling . . . **BRAZEN VIRTUE** by Nora Roberts.

The steamy summer streets of Washington are no match for the phone lines of Fantasy, Inc., where every man's dreams come true. The "hotline" works perfectly for its anonymous clients and the teachers and housewives who moonlight as call girls . . . until a brilliant madman plugs in with twisted passion. Introducing GRACE McCABE, a gorgeous bestselling mystery writer determined to trap her sister's killer, and ED JACKSON, the handsome and tenacious cop you first met in **SACRED SINS.**
(continued)

We have more thrilling news for you. We're going to run a fabulous, fun contest throughout our Fifth Year called the "Hometown Hunk Contest." We will reissue six marvelous LOVESWEPT's (by six marvelous authors, of course) that were first published in the early days. The titles and authors are:

IN A CLASS BY ITSELF by Sandra Brown
FOR THE LOVE OF SAMI by Fayrene Preston
C.J.'S FATE by Kay Hooper
THE LADY AND THE UNICORN by Iris Johansen
CHARADE by Joan Elliot Pickart
DARLING OBSTACLES by Barbara Boswell

In the backs of our June, July, and August LOVESWEPTs we will publish "cover notes" just like those we use here at Bantam to create covers. These notes will describe the heroine and hero, give a teaser on the plot, and suggest a scene from the book for the cover. Your part in the contest will be to see if a great looking man in your own hometown fits our description and your ideas about what the hero of one of these books looks like. If so, you enter him in the contest (contest blanks will be in the books starting month-after-next, too), along with his picture. The "hometown hunk" who is selected will be the model for a new cover of the book! We hope you'll find absolutely great looking men who are just perfect for the covers of these six great LOVESWEPTs. We can't wait to start judging those pictures! Indeed, a dozen women in the company who've heard about the contest are just begging to help open the mail!

And now for our terrific romances next month!

She started it all with LOVESWEPT #1, **HEAVEN'S PRICE**—Sandra Brown. And, naturally, we asked Sandra to lead off our Fifth Birthday list. Now you can relish **ADAM'S FALL**, LOVESWEPT #252, the thrilling story that brings back two great characters from **FANTA C**. Heroine Lilah Mason is challenged like she's never been before when she encounters ADAM CAVANAUGH again. Adam's down, but not out, flat on his back—yet he and Lilah learn he can still fall!

And, now it is a great pleasure to introduce two talented writers making their debuts with LOVESWEPT.

First, we have Tami Hoag presenting us with **THE TROUBLE WITH J.J.**, LOVESWEPT #253. Here's all the humor and heartwarming romance of two great people—lovely Genna Hastings and devastating J.J. Hennessy. She's the adorable lady next door; he's her new neighbor with rippling muscles and mile-wide shoulders. A don't miss read, for sure!

Next, there's **THE GRAND FINALE**, LOVESWEPT #254, by Janet Evanovich. **THE GRAND FINALE** is riotously funny and in the opening chapter pizza tycoon Berry Knudsen literally falls for tall, dark, muscular Jake Sawyer. She didn't really mean to, but somehow she got a perfect view of the perfect man through

(continued)

his bedroom window! Jake doesn't have her arrested for peeping because he's having too much fun watching her squirm as she tries to explain herself!

HOLD ON TIGHT, LOVESWEPT #255, is Deborah Smith's second book for us. You'll remember that her first was a wonderful island fantasy. **HOLD ON TIGHT**, a very different but equally strong love story, shows Deborah's range. It's set in both a small Southern town, and the big city of Birmingham and features sophisticated Dinah Sheridan, a former beauty queen turned politician wooed by Rucker McClure, an irreverent bestselling journalist/author. As Deborah says "the teasing, provocative Rucker McClure is just about as sexy as a man can get!" We're sure that you won't want to let go of **HOLD ON TIGHT.**

Josh Long's men—and his lovely wife, Raven—are back to help out one of Kay Hooper's most devastatingly sexy heroes ever in **OUTLAW DEREK**, LOVESWEPT #256. A beguiling and beautiful woman wanders into the life of a longtime loner and sets him on fire with love. In the midst of danger, Derek Ross gentles the sweet spirit of Shannon Brown in one of Kay's most memorable and touching romances ever.

And last, but never, never least is our own Iris Johansen, who will return next August to celebrate *her* fifth anniversary as a published author. Iris has created for us a very special birthday present, **MAN FROM HALF MOON BAY**, LOVESWEPT #257. Surprise. Panic. Then desire like an electric shock filled Sara O'Rourke when she saw Jordan Bandor across the crowded room. For eighteen months she'd lived free of the man from the harsh, unforgiving Australian outback who'd swept her off her feet, then wrapped her in a seductive web of sensual pleasure that left no room for work or friends. And now these two passionate people must work out their relationship in an atmosphere of desperate danger!

We started LOVESWEPT in a marketplace full of romances. Some said we'd never last. But we've been here for five happy years because of *your* support. Thank you from the bottom of our hearts, and here's to five more wonderful years!

Carolyn Nichols

Carolyn Nichols
   Editor

LOVESWEPT
Bantam Books
666 Fifth Avenue
New York, NY 10103

The first Delaney trilogy

Heirs to a great dynasty, the Delaney brothers were united by blood, united by devotion to their rugged land . . . and known far and wide as

THE SHAMROCK TRINITY

Bantam's bestselling LOVESWEPT romance line built its reputation on quality and innovation. Now, a remarkable and unique event in romance publishing comes from the same source: THE SHAMROCK TRINITY, three daringly original novels written by three of the most successful women's romance writers today. Kay Hooper, Iris Johansen, and Fayrene Preston have created a trio of books that are dynamite love stories bursting with strong, fascinating male and female characters, deeply sensual love scenes, the humor for which LOVESWEPT is famous, and a deliciously fresh approach to romance writing.

THE SHAMROCK TRINITY—Burke, York, and Rafe: Powerful men . . . rakes and charmers . . . they needed only love to make their lives complete.

☐ *RAFE, THE MAVERICK by Kay Hooper*

Rafe Delaney was a heartbreaker whose ebony eyes held laughing devils and whose lilting voice could charm any lady—or any horse—until a stallion named Diablo left him in the dust. It took Maggie O'Riley to work her magic on the impossible horse . . . and on his bold owner. Maggie's grace and strength made Rafe yearn to share the raw beauty of his land with her, to teach her the exquisite pleasure of yielding to the heat inside her. Maggie was stirred by Rafe's passion, but would his reputation and her ambition keep their kindred spirits apart?   (21846 • $2.75)

LOVESWEPT

□ YORK, THE RENEGADE by Iris Johansen

Some men were made to fight dragons, Sierra Smith thought when she first met York Delaney. The rebel brother had roamed the world for years before calling the rough mining town of Hell's Bluff home. Now, the spirited young woman who'd penetrated this renegade's paradise had awakened a savage and tender possessiveness in York: something he never expected to find in himself. Sierra had known loneliness and isolation too—enough to realize that York's restlessness had only to do with finding a place to belong. Could she convince him that love was such a place, that the refuge he'd always sought was in her arms?

(21847 • $2.75)

□ BURKE, THE KINGPIN by Fayrene Preston

Cara Winston appeared as a fantasy, racing on horseback to catch the day's last light—her silver hair glistening, her dress the color of the Arizona sunset . . . and Burke Delaney wanted her. She was on his horse, on his land: she would have to belong to him too. But Cara was quicksilver, impossible to hold, a wild creature whose scent was midnight flowers and sweet grass. Burke had always taken what he wanted, by willing it or fighting for it; Cara cherished her freedom and refused to believe his love would last. Could he make her see he'd captured her to have and hold forever?

(21848 • $2.75)